To Have and to Hold

BETWEEN THE SHEETS

TRICIA ADAMS

SECOND CHANCE AT LOVE
BOOK

BETWEEN THE SHEETS

Copyright © 1984 by Tricia Adams

All rights reserved. No part of this publication may be reproduced or
transmitted in any form or by any means, electronic or mechanical,
including photocopy, recording, or any information storage and re-
trieval system, without permission in writing from the publisher.

Requests for permission to make copies of any part of the work should
be mailed to: Permissions, To Have and to Hold, The Berkley Publishing Group, 200 Madison Avenue, New York, NY 10016.

First edition published April 1984

First printing

"Second Chance at Love," the butterfly emblem, and "To Have and
to Hold" are trademarks belonging to Jove Publications, Inc.

Printed in the United States of America

To Have and to Hold books are published by
The Berkley Publishing Group
200 Madison Avenue, New York, NY 10016

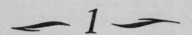

1

CLEA WITHERSPOON BOTTINGTON was actually quite pleased that Mitch had canceled their luncheon date in favor of one of his interminable board meetings. But, of course, it wouldn't do to show any emotion, either positive or negative, in front of his secretary. Instead she smiled politely at Miss Hoven, who waited, pencil poised, to see if there was any reply to the dictated message.

"Tell my husband I'll see him at dinner," Clea stated in her well-modulated finishing school voice. However, she knew, and Miss Hoven knew, that Mitch missed dinner five nights out of seven. As president of Klectronics International, he seldom turned down an opportunity to conduct business—even if that business kept him away from home.

After eight years of marriage, Clea had learned to accept that fact with equanimity. Not that she had any cause for complaint. As a Bottington, of *the* Bottingtons, she had everything money could buy. Plus a family genealogy—Mitch's—that went impeccably back to pre-Revolutionary days. Which was as it should be, since Clea's own Witherspoon ancestry was also impeccable, with roots going back almost as far as her husband's.

Miss Hoven efficiently jotted down Clea's message, then looked up to see if there were any additions. A quick flash of envy glimmered in the older woman's eye as she scrutinized Clea's new sable-trimmed suede coat, an envy that was just as quickly concealed, although not before Clea had noticed it. For some reason, this caused Clea to say, "Could you please sign it 'Love.'" And when Miss Hoven did so, without comment, Clea waved farewell, the large diamond on her ring finger catching the light from the chandelier overhead.

Gliding smoothly across the plush carpet, she left the office, feeling no need to glance in the entry-hall mirror. She knew without looking that every ash-blond hair was perfectly in place and that her makeup was just as fresh-looking as when she'd left the house. A Bottington wouldn't be found dead with smeared lipstick or a shred of lacy slip showing. It was extremely important, as Mitch often reminded her, to present a totally proper image when facing the public.

With grace born of long practice, Clea exited the building, her measured steps those of a socialite looking forward to another leisurely day of couturier shopping. This pace endured until Clea reached her silver-gray Rolls Royce. But once she was behind the wheel an almost imperceptible, totally improper, gleam of mischief shone in her wide hazel eyes. Mitch's absence from lunch gave her an entirely free afternoon to work on the opening chapter of her book. And she had just had the most marvelous idea for a new scene.

The Rolls purred into action, but it didn't move in the direction of the couturiers or Hampstead Estates. Instead, Clea steered it to a row of rather dilapidated Victorian houses that had long since been turned into apartments. Pulling up in front of the best-looking of the lot, a three-story building newly repainted a cheerful lavender with white curlique trim, she turned off the ignition and hastily grabbed a package that bore the name of a trendy designer. This made excellent camouflage. For inside was an odd assortment of research materials, collected in the most surreptitious manner, and absolutely essential to the task at hand.

Removing her coat, Clea folded it carefully, tucked it in the well beneath the passenger seat, then covered it with a well-worn multicolored afghan. Shivering slightly, she put on a pale blue double-knit sweater and covered her stylishly coiffed hair with a paisley cotton scarf. It was probably unnecessary to take such elaborate precautions, she thought, feeling slightly foolish. Yet she couldn't risk being recognized by a chance visitor to the apartment house. Dressed simply, Clea looked, she hoped, like any working girl returning home for a quick meal after doing a bit of splurge shopping. The thought almost made her grin. This game of pretend, in her very proper, very routine world, was actually quite amusing.

She locked the car, double-checked the doors, then glanced around and decided everything was satisfactory. With an almost girlish twitch of her slim hips, hips that belied her thirty years, as did her flawless cameo complexion, she kept keys in hand and proceeded up the front steps of the apartment building. Nodding to Professor Tanners, another tenant, she said her usual friendly but noninvitational hello. Mr. Tanners, tall, dark-haired, distinguished, and on staff at a nearby college, doffed his hat and nodded back. Although the two never actually spoke, they'd come to recognize each other in passing, and by inbred courtesy they acknowledged this recognition.

Climbing the single flight of curving ecru-carpeted

stairs, Clea came to her apartment, opened the door, closed it behind her, and heaved a sigh of relief. Safe at last in her own private world. Technically speaking, of course, nothing could be more private than the white-columned, barred-gate mansion in which she lived; but this was private in a different, very special way, because it was hers alone. Nobody knew she had rented the studio. Nobody knew she visited it twice a week, and even more often whenever possible. It was a secret sanctuary where she could look out on the world, but no one could look in on her.

Clea made herself a pot of coffee and checked the small refrigerator for food. There was still some Camembert, a few crackers, a shiny red apple, and a tiny bunch of darkest purple grapes. Perfect. Much better than eating at the crowded restaurant she would have gone to with Mitch, a restaurant chosen not for the excellence of its food but for its convenience to his office and the speed with which he could eat and run—right back to his work.

Always work, Clea thought. Mitch was married to his work. When she first met him he had been at Stanford earning his master's degree in business administration. Doing well, grade-wise, of course, as befitted a Bottington scion, but also making quite a hit on the campus social scene.

Her roommate, Hillary, had introduced them on a blind date, and at very first sight Clea could understand the reason for his popularity among the campus coeds. Mitch was tall, over six feet, and his broad shoulders and long, muscular legs were artfully emphasized by a white turtleneck sweater and tailored navy slacks. Dark wavy hair fell boyishly across his forehead, gray eyes mocked under dark lashes, and a knowing grin seemed a permanent part of his sensuous, softly curving mouth.

The grin had been turned on her full force, and it just

about melted her bones. Clea could still remember that evening. She had stood there, gaping, a conscientious product of her senior year at an exclusive girls-only finishing school. She had worn, she recalled, a perfectly plain, extraordinarily expensive, black spaghetti-strap dress, black heels, a thin gold pendant around her neck. Her blond hair was swept off to one side, an attempt to make herself look as sophisticated as possible. After all, Mitchell Bottington was easily the best catch around, Hillary had informed her. Hillary would have grabbed him herself, so she said, if only she weren't already "engaged to be engaged" to someone else.

Clea had been out with a number of boys, none of them too sophisticated despite their bold talk and pretend bravado. But Mitch was clearly a man, and his talk and bravado were for real. So Clea had fallen in love, right then and there. And if she hadn't been so determined to remain a virgin until her wedding night, Mitch's persistent advances would have easily overwhelmed her. As it was, she returned to the dorm that first evening, and every evening after that, still shaking from the strain of repressing what had quickly become an insistent and growing bonfire within her loins.

Fortunately, Mitch proposed before her resolve could totally weaken. Their wedding was one of the most extravagant in San Francisco history. And the honeymoon that followed . . . well, Clea thought Mitch was wonderful. She still thought so.

She had gotten pregnant almost immediately, settling, after Kevin's birth, into her expected role as socialite matron, head of a household replete with a nanny for the baby, plus the requisite maids. An excellent hostess, she organized an endless round of superb dinner parties. Mitch, naturally, was working for his father. But the young couple still found lots of time to spend together, time to share jokes and gossip, long hours for love and laughter. It had seemed the best life possible, the only life possible.

But then, when Kevin was two, Mitch's father had died, and Mitch took over Klectronics—or rather Klectronics seemed to take him over.

As the years passed, Clea saw less and less of her husband. The change was so gradual that she almost didn't notice it. After all, it was to be expected that the head of an international business would be thoroughly involved in it. And it went without saying that his wife would embrace her proper role as homemaker and mother.

So Clea had felt fulfilled, and this fulfillment had lasted until Kevin went to kindergarten, then first grade with it's all-day schedule. She tried to get pregnant again, but without success. Doctors could find nothing wrong and said it was just one of those things. Maybe she would have felt less empty if Mitch had been home more. But he wasn't, and she felt she had no right to make him choose between her and his work.

Enough of that, Clea thought abruptly. Pulling over a cushion-padded chair, she sat down at her typewriter, piling up the prerequisite stack of clean white paper nearby. She looked at her notes, put her fingers on the keys, and started her umpteenth draft of page ten. Her heroine, Tanya, had just walked into the main office of Tony's construction firm. Tanya was an architect, and her plans for the remodeling of a socialite's home had been altered without permission once too often. This arrogant, macho man was about to be put in his place. She would no longer tolerate being treated like some interloper, a scatterbrained female whose opinion didn't count.

"Do I have to buy you glasses, or is it just that you need remedial reading classes?" Tanya exploded, throw-

ing a sheaf of rolled-up drawings on his desk.

"Do you realize that rhymes?" Tony said with amusement, not even glancing at the drawings. "Maybe you should have been a poet instead of an architect. A much more feminine profession, by the way."

Tanya could feel her face flush up to the roots of her short-cropped red hair. Tony Bernardo always managed to make her feel like an absolute idiot. And it didn't help any that he kept staring at her khaki jumpsuit as if he could see through it to the curves underneath. Not only was it mortifying, it also reminded her that she definitely did have curves underneath.

"Why don't you grow up?" Tanya retorted, well aware of her inability to ignore the perverse magnetic attraction that seemed to intensify each time she met this lout. "Feminine women are architects, doctors, and lawyers these days. And only cave-clunk types like you are too dense to recognize it."

Clea stopped typing and smiled. No female in her right mind would be attracted to a walking stud who wanted to see her permanently installed behind a kitchen sink. But then, this was fantasy fiction and sandy-haired, dark-eyed, barrel-chested Tony was the perfect fantasy hero, an obvious sexual dynamo. Tanya, the ice-maiden intellectual, was going to have quite a problem with him.

Staring out the apartment's picture window at a row of poplar trees, Clea paused for a moment to reflect on how she'd gotten involved with this foolishness in the first place.

She recalled the circumstances quite clearly. Mitch had been away on a business trip, as usual, and Kevin was sound asleep. Clea had stood over her son for several minutes, wondering how anybody who was such a little devil all day could seem so angelic at night. She had an urge to wake him, just to have someone to talk to, but of course she didn't.

Loneliness crept in, and on its heels, boredom. She had picked up a new fashion magazine, flipped through the pages, found nothing of interest, put it down. She had already read everything else in the house of even remote appeal, and it was only nine o'clock. Perhaps a cup of tea and some English biscuits might help her sleep.

Walking downstairs to the kitchen, Clea put the gleaming kettle on to boil and reached into the cupboard for the biscuit tin. On top of the colorfully decorated container was a slim paperback book with an equally vivid cover featuring a young man and woman in smoldering embrace against a lush background of hibiscus and frangipani. The book bore the title *Cupid's Arrow.*

Almost absentmindedly Clea had picked it up, making a mental note to tell the new maid not to leave her personal belongings about. And then, just as absentmindedly, Clea began to thumb through the pages as she sipped her steaming herbal brew.

Two hours later she had completed the novel. How can anybody write that trash, much less read it? she had wondered, placing the book back where she'd found it. And if her dreams that night were a little more lovely, crystal bells tinkling against the solitary darkness of her king-sized bed, Clea had forgotten them by morning.

A few days later, by sheer coincidence, Clea attended a by-invitation-only fashion show. The woman sitting next to her was only a casual acquaintance, but a Bottington could not sit next to somebody without at least an attempt at polite conversation. After all, there was the family image to uphold. So small talk passed back and forth, and during its course the woman jokingly mentioned that she had become addicted to romance novels. "I read at least one a week, sometimes two," she admitted offhandedly.

Without really thinking, Clea responded that she had just read her first one, and that she really thought any grammar school child could have come up with the plot. Although, of course, this particular book was perhaps an exception, she added, softening her words as she took in her companion's irate expression.

But the woman was not so easily mollified. "If you think they're so easy to write," she responded tartly, "why don't you try it?"

"Maybe I will." Clea had laughed, changing the subject as an absolutely stunning beaded gown was paraded on the runway. But the conversation stuck in her mind that afternoon as she drove home to her servant-occupied house. She continued to think about it at odd moments during the ensuing days until, nagged by she didn't know what, Clea found herself at a bookstore picking up several of the more luridly covered romance books that dominated the shelves.

From there it was all systems go. She could easily, she assured herself, do better. But it wasn't as easy as she'd thought. Not easy at all. In fact, it was turning out to be quite difficult.

Clea recommenced typing.

"You wouldn't be so frustrated if you spent a little time in the sack with somebody who knew what he was doing," Tony retorted sardonically.

Tanya picked up a paperweight from the desk and flung it at her tormentor. It would have hit him on the cheek if he hadn't quickly shifted position. Before she could reach for another missile, Tony was at her side, pulling her toward him.

At this point, Clea knew, there had to be a sensuous scene. This would be her fourth attempt to describe Tony's demanding mouth on Tanya's resisting lips. Darn, double darn. She couldn't come up with three erotic sentences, much less three paragraphs or the preferred full page.

Once again Clea turned to the stack of "reference" books beside her small desk. One had been written by a noted woman of the streets. Another was filled with vivid descriptions of a woman's sexual fantasies, a third with male fantasies. And a fourth offered rather clinical advice on "how to improve one's sex life after marriage."

Clea's hazel eyes widened as she perused the material. She had never heard of such goings on. Did women really admit to wanting such bedroom intimacies? Did men really do those things? Certainly Mitch didn't. He was so tired when he came home that the standard missionary position was the most he could manage. And it was all so quickly over and done with, as if he were dictating a letter that had to get out immediately.

Clea managed to fill a few more pages with words, turning frequently to her thesaurus to look up synonyms for *virile* and *desire*. Afternoon storm clouds now filled the picture window and she had only accomplished half of her ten-page goal. And even those five pages were less than satisfactory.

Covering the typewriter, Clea frowned. Why was she having so much trouble? After all, everybody knew what went on when a man and woman were physically attracted to each other. Or did they?

Tapping her long, beautifully manicured fingernails on the desk, she felt the surge of frustration that had become all too familiar since she'd started writing the book. Maybe everybody else knew, but she clearly didn't. It had been such a long time since she'd felt an overwhelming sexual urge, and her lack of experience in expressing her needs combined with Mitch's increasing reserve was enough to cause a total creative block. If she really wanted to write this stuff, she would have to get some "hands-on" knowledge. But from where?

Clea briefly considered the possibility of having an affair. Very briefly. It was out of the question. Besides, she loved her husband. It was just that he was so . . . well, staid.

Perhaps she could ask a friend for information. No, that was equally unthinkable. She could just hear herself asking someone like Amelia Vandergrif to describe her sexual relationship with Hunter Kenworthy, her fiancé. Just the hint would cause a scandal, and wasn't avoiding scandal the reason she had rented this apartment? That and the desire to keep her efforts secret from Mitch.

Which brought her thoughts full circle, right back to Mitch. Clea rinsed out the coffeepot, placed her crumpled sheets of typing paper and coffee grounds in a paper bag to be deposited in the trash bin downstairs. All the while her mind kept darting this way and that. Mitchell Bottington. Mitchell Eduard Bottington. Mitchell Eduard Bottington, president of Klectronics International. Mitchell Eduard Bottington who looked like a magazine centerfold and spent a lot more time at his desk than he did in bed.

Fine way to think of your husband, Clea mused. A husband doing his best to provide for his family, his best to keep up the Bottington image, his best to keep up the Klectronics image. Clea locked the apartment door behind her, still thinking about her need for some advanced sex education. She thought some more as she got into the Rolls Royce, switched into her much warmer fur-trimmed coat, turned on the ignition, and drove through the now crowded streets of San Francisco. No way around it, Mitch would have to do. But how? And when?

He still wasn't home by 10 P.M. Kevin had long since gone to bed. A note on the antique mahogany entry room table, written by the maid, had informed her that Mitch was "tied up in an emergency conference," but that had been hours ago. It was always a conference. If it wasn't, it was an informal business meeting over drinks and dinner which would formally result in a multimillion-dollar contract. Or it was stacks of paperwork, too heavy, too technical to be brought home.

Once again, Clea went to bed alone, clad in her white satin pajamas, her face lightly creamed, a net over her hair to protect the style that had to be artfully arranged in two-hour sessions at the beauty salon every three days. She read a portion of another romance novel that she kept by her bedside—feeling totally frustrated in more ways than one—and finally fell into restless slumber, images of Tony Bernardo flashing through her dreams.

When she awoke the next morning later than usual, Mitch had already left. Thus, he missed the smile of perverse glee that illuminated his wife's face as an idea came to her out of the blue, like a light coming on suddenly after a fuse had been put in place.

"If Mitch it has to be, then Mitch it is going to be," Clea said out loud, her hazel eyes sparkling in a way that made her look like a mischievous adolescent. "I'll make him notice me again, even if I have to experiment with a different chapter from my reference books every single night."

That afternoon, and the one following, Clea didn't go near her clandestine apartment. Instead she went shopping at the lingerie department of Neiman-Marcus, trying on an assortment of sexy nightgowns that made her blush each time she looked in the dressing-room mirror. Settling on a lacy lavender peignoir and nightgown that displayed much more than it covered, Clea paid for it in cash rather than risk having the salesclerk recognize the Bottington name on her charge card. She followed the same procedure in a small perfumerie a few blocks away, after asking in somewhat embarrassed tones for a fragrance "guaranteed to tempt a monk."

Once home, she was tempted to place lingerie and

perfume back in their respective boxes and donate them, anonymously, to a local thrift shop. But she resisted the impulse. Instead, she telephoned Mitch's office and asked Miss Hoven what time he would be home that evening. "I've got a very special meal prepared for him," she added, trying to sound as nonchalant as possible.

Miss Hoven, as usual, put her on "hold." Clea didn't particularly like her husband's secretary. The woman's overly efficient manner always made her feel like an intruder. That, combined with the fact that Miss Hoven got to spend eight hours a day with Mitch while she was lucky to get half an hour, was more than enough cause for irritation. But tonight she was going to have more than half an hour: Mitch wasn't disappearing anyplace except to their bedroom after dinner. Clea didn't care if she had to hog-tie him. And she sincerely hoped it would be easier than that. Much easier. It should be, shouldn't it? Unless the man were wearing blinders and a nose plug.

Glancing at the Tiffany watch on her slim wrist, Clea noted that three minutes had passed. She half expected to hear Miss Hoven's brisk voice inform her that "Mr. Bottington is tied up in a meeting." But, to her amazement, the voice that finally came on the line belonged to her seldom-seen spouse.

"Hi, honey, what's up? Miss Hoven told me you had an urgent message and that I had better discuss it with you personally."

With a wave of irritation, Clea wondered why the secretary had put it that way. Now her invitation to an "intimate dinner à deux" would sound like an insignificant blip on the horizon of importance. One of these days she would get her revenge, but at the moment she was more interested in getting Mitch out of the office.

"You sound cheerful," she commented, making her voice as light as possible.

"I have reason to be," Mitch responded, his deep baritone holding more than a hint of satisfaction. "You remember that deal with the German firm I told you about? Well it looks like it's finally going to come through. I'm tempted to let the word leak out today; that would do wonders for Klectronics' stock."

Mitch's elation gave Clea just the opening she needed. "Darling, has there ever been a time when you put your mind to accomplishing something that didn't come to pass? Your father would be justifiably proud of you, and it gives us even more reason to celebrate."

There was a brief pause, and she could almost see Mitch wondering what on earth she was talking about. So before he could question her, she hastily cooed, "Oh dear, there's someone here to show me some revised plans for the kitchen remodeling. I just wanted to make certain you'd be home by seven for the special meal I've personally prepared. Kevin's got other plans, so it will be just the two of us. You will come, won't you? Please?"

"Clea, I'm piled up to the ceiling with paperwork. If I get home before midnight, I'll consider myself lucky." Mitch had the grace to sound somewhat apologetic, and under normal circumstances Clea might have backed down. But she hadn't bought that nightgown and perfume for nothing, and nothing was what she was going to get if she allowed herself to retreat.

"Pretty please, darling," she said in a somewhat woebegone tone. "I've fussed over this meal all day and it's very important that you be here to share it with me. It's not as if I ask for an extra hour of your time very often."

Her words were deliberately calculated to make him feel guilty, and as such, they succeeded. "You're right, Clea," he said. "I don't spend enough time with you and Kevin. If it's so important to you, I'll make it home by seven, one way or another. Even if it means returning to the office late tonight to finish up this contract revision."

Before Mitch would think twice about his promise, Clea bid him a hasty farewell. She wondered what had made her say anything about a kitchen remodeling. Their enormous kitchen had been completely redone three years ago and was perfectly satisfactory. Oh well, she would come up with something that needed refinement. A new set of cabinets, perhaps. It wasn't really a problem, since Mitch always enjoyed watching her spend the money he earned. Right now she had only to think of a way to convince Kevin he wanted to spend the night at a friend's house. Her seven-year-old was a delightful child, but his idea of fun was getting Daddy to play with their home computer and that wasn't exactly the type of game Clea had in mind.

Fortunately, when she picked Kevin up from school—it was her turn for carpool duty—he was accompanied by his "almost best friend," Boppo.

"Guess what, Mom?" Kevin exclaimed, running up to the car dragging the rather pudgy Boppo behind him. Without waiting for his mother to guess, he said, "Boppo got the neatest birthday present from his godfather and it's got . . ." Kevin went on to detail the numerous attractions of the gift, which sounded like a cross between a space ship assembly kit and a model car collision course.

Yes, she would drive him to Boppo's house. Yes, he could have dinner with Boppo's family at the Alabama Fried Chicken place. And yes, he most certainly could spend the night.

Yes, yes, yes, Clea thought happily as she waved good-bye to her son. Looking like a miniature businessman in his tailored blue slacks and white shirt—de rigueur attire at the exclusive Country Day School he attended—Kevin waved happily back. Suddenly aware of the sandy-blonde curls dripping down over her son's forehead, Clea made a mental note to set up an appointment for a haircut.

But not now. Now was for telling the nanny she could have the evening off to visit her sick sister; the reaction to this was so appreciative that Clea extended the leave of absence into the following day.

Now was for telephoning a very discreet catering service that specialized in preparing "home-cooked" meals for wealthy women whose culinary capabilities left something to be desired but who, for various reasons, wished to appear adroit in the kitchen. Satisfied that the aroma of freshly baked bread would soon be filling her house, Clea was free to turn her attentions to the scheme at hand. A scheme that began with a long, luxurious bubble bath.

2

AFTER ALMOST FALLING asleep in the custom-designed black marble step-in tub, Clea finally emerged, toweled herself dry, and then began dabbing musk oil on every pulse spot, every erogenous zone. The seductive peignoir and nightgown followed, so transparent that she decided to temporarily cover them with a much warmer bathrobe.

Releasing her hair from its confining pins, she let it fall, golden waves on alabaster shoulders. Her flawless skin, flushed from the heat of the tub, needed no makeup, and she added none except for a mere touch of pastel shadow that made her eyes look like opalescent. More than satisfied with her appearance, Clea curled up in a green damask armchair and began another chapter from the book on women's sexual fantasies, her fair brows rising from time to time as she came across a particularly steamy passage.

Downstairs, the grandfather clock chimed seven. At seven-fifteen she heard Mitch's key in the door. She heard him wandering around, hanging up his coat, putting down his ever-present briefcase, performing the myriad and one rituals that marked each evening's homecoming. In a few minutes, she knew, he would go to the liquor cabinet, and pour himself a scotch on the rocks. And that was when she'd make her grand entrance.

Tucking her erotic reading material under a stack of lingerie in a dresser drawer, Clea removed her heavy robe and slippers. On impulse she added a dab of perfume to each ankle, and then she took a deep breath and started slowly down the stairs.

Watching Mitch from the shadowy sanctuary of the living-room doorway, Clea noticed how tired he looked. It had been a very long day, and she'd bet he hadn't stopped, even to take a coffee break. Yet even with the circles under his smoke-gray eyes, the half-knotted silk tie, the white shirt, sagging somewhat after confinement under the de rigueur blue suit, he still looked fantastic. Clea wished he needed her more, that she could go to him and give him a sympathetic hug.

She repressed all such maternal instincts, however. Mitch would hardly appreciate them. He had an intense aversion to leaning on anyone for support. He was so damn independent. She loved that independence, but sometimes it could be a thorough pain.

Clea shivered in her thin negligee, then braced herself for action. She was either going to stand there and stare or she was going to get on with her plan and let the chips fall where they may.

"Hello, Mitch," she murmured softly, squaring her slim shoulders as if to bolster herself for the job ahead.

"Hi, hon," Mitch replied without turning around, pouring the amber liquid into a glistening brandy snifter, holding it up to the light, and then taking a swift gulp.

Clea pushed back a twinge of annoyance. "Aren't you

going to kiss me?" she asked, making her tone as light as possible.

Mitch sighed wearily. "It's been a tough day," he stated. "Rodriggs came in with a bid that was way under actual costs, and it's due tomorrow. Which means I have to go back tonight and redo the whole complicated mess with him. Rodriggs is a top-drawer analyst, but lately he's gotten much too optimistic."

Mitch was still staring at the brandy snifter, facing away from her toward the natural stone fireplace that occupied an entire wall of the living room. Clea, in turn, was staring at the broad muscles across his back, the slim hips, the long legs that had brought him so speedily to the goal post during their college days. For a man who spent most of his days pushing a pen, with only occasional visits to the gym, he had a marvelous body. In fact, Clea thought somewhat lecherously, marvelous was an understatement.

She walked silently across the plush cocoa shag carpet and put her arms around his waist, leaning her face against his shoulder blades to feel the warmth emanating from him like a welcoming beacon.

"Can't you skip Rodriggs tonight," she whispered, the words almost lost in the soft folds of his shirt. "I really would like . . . well, to be with you."

Mitch tensed. She felt it like a warning signal. "Clea, I'm exhausted. I wouldn't be going back to the office if I didn't have to. Even if I stayed home, I wouldn't be good for much. Can't you find something else to keep you occupied?"

This time it was Clea's turn to tense, and without knowing quite why, or maybe she did, she replied, "Well, yes, I can find something else to keep me occupied. I can walk down Market Street in my new outfit. An outfit you haven't even bothered to look at yet."

"Okay," Mitch replied, a teasing edge to his voice. "I'll look. Just to see what I'm missing..." He pivoted to face her, bent to give the customary brief reunion kiss, and ran his hands absently along her hips. When the hands touched sheer lace instead of the expected wool slacks, they stopped short.

Mitch's eyes widened. Clea could see flecks of amber in the sea of gray as his dark brows raised in complete astonishment. His hands started moving again, traveling lightly across her barely covered buttocks. And then he stepped back and stared.

"Like it?" Clea asked provocatively, pirouetting gracefully before him.

"What the hell is that?" he asked, staring at the apparition before him, a very unbusinesslike blush rising from his open shirt collar and moving rapidly up to his wavy hairline.

"A negligee," Clea replied, laughter bubbling up in her throat. "Can't you tell? Or have you been confined to Klectronics' bachelor quarters too long?" Mitch's very rare blushes never ceased to amaze her. Her husband, so distinguished, so prominent, so world-traveled, could still redden involuntarily at an unexpected smutty remark or a too revealing outfit.

"Doesn't look like a negligee to me," Mitch stated firmly, his eyes riveted to the rose-tipped breasts almost totally visible through the filmy lavender lace. "It looks more like a transparent doily with a few extra holes. Did you buy it, or did someone give it to you in hopes that you would catch pneumonia and mention him in your will?"

"Very funny," Clea countered, raising one eyebrow to indicate she didn't think it was funny at all. "For your information, not only did I buy it, but you paid for it—and quite a lot too."

"But there's nothing there," Mitch protested.

Clea moved toward him and ran her fingers gently across his slightly parted lips. "Do be a sweetheart and tell me it's becoming. I mean, it is, isn't it?"

Mitch's craggy face appeared almost stern. "Clea," he said warningly, "this isn't at all like you. What's up?"

"Well, I hoped it was going to be you," she replied huskily, letting her hand drop down to trail over the hollow of his stomach.

"Clea, I told you——" Clea stopped him in mid-sentence by standing on tiptoe, reaching around his neck, and pulling his mouth down upon hers. Mitch's resistance lasted exactly three seconds. It didn't have a chance against her probing tongue. His own tongue moved swiftly out to meet the tantalizing touch of the darting intruder.

When they finally parted, she happily noted his dilated pupils, his speculative look; he was staring at her body as if he'd never seen it before. She could also see what she wanted to see, what she had felt during their embrace——the hard bulge of masculinity that even his tailored slacks couldn't conceal.

Round one to the lady in the sexy nightie, she thought, her mind working, click, click, like an abacus. If she was going to play this right, she'd have to keep her mind on the game, not on the opponent.

She smiled slightly as her gaze dropped deliberately and pointedly downward, then up toward Mitch's face. "If you think this is a doily, you ought to see the table underneath," she invited, removing the peignoir slowly and letting it drop to her bare feet.

She heard Mitch's breath catch and saw the spreading blush that made him seem like a schoolboy caught in the act of peeping through the headmistress's window. "You're a good-looking woman," he said eventually, standing there as if rooted permanently to the spot.

"I feel good too," Clea drawled. "Why don't you see for yourself?"

For the briefest of intervals, Mitch's eyes flickered. But then he drew his long dark lashes over them like a hood. Damn his self-control, Clea fumed silently.

"Hon, I've got to go back to the office tonight." The tone was firm, unwavering.

"I didn't say you shouldn't go back to the office tonight," Clea countered, her tone equally unwavering. "I just hoped you might delay your departure a bit. Not very long. Just long enough to spend a few private moments with your adoring wife."

When Mitch didn't reply, she shrugged, letting the spaghetti strap on one ivory shoulder slip down along her arm. Then she knelt in front of him to pick up the peignoir, bending deliberately forward so he could get an unimpeded view of her swelling breasts. Her husband's large hands were clenched into tight fists.

When Clea arose, her hazel eyes were cool, almost distant. She slowly put on the peignoir, then walked toward the liquor cabinet, poured herself a brandy, and offered him a solitary toast. "Maybe someone on Market Street will appreciate me more," she goaded, taking a stinging sip from the crystal glass, her expression remote.

"What the hell are you trying to do?" Mitch growled, his voice taut with barely restrained fury.

"Nothing. Absolutely nothing. At least not with my husband." She emphasized the word *husband,* hoping the suggestion that she might search for a substitute would spur him to action.

"Clea, for crying out loud," Mitch protested. "I've got exactly three million dollars resting on this deal. That's not a sum to be sneezed at."

"By all means, restrain that sneeze," Clea retorted. "After all, if there's anything we're short of, it's money in the bank." Her glance swept the plush room deliberately, taking in the expensive antique furniture, the Tiffany lamps, the signed oil paintings displayed against the flocked wallpaper.

This time her shrug was even more eloquent, more dismissive. When the nightgown strap fell from her shoulder, she pulled it quickly back into place. She ran her fingers through her loosely waved ash-blond hair, pulling it away from her high cheekbones in a casual, taunting gesture.

Mitch's blush had long since disappeared, and his lips were compressed in a thin line. "What the hell has gotten into you?" he asked harshly.

"Certainly not you," Clea retorted. "At least not in a long time."

"That's not true, and that's not what I meant."

"I know what you meant. And I know what I mean." Her tone was cutting, a switchblade aimed where it could hurt the most. What Mitch had no way of knowing was that it hurt her also. But she had to get him angry enough to make a move in her direction. The game had become real life. There was no way Mitch was going to leave her tonight. For if he did, her ego cried, she might very well head out for Market Street after all.

Silence descended like a shroud. When Mitch spun around and picked up his jacket from the couch without another word, Clea's head rose like a wounded doe's. She finished her brandy in one swift gulp and walked briskly toward the doorway, not even bothering to glance back over her shoulder.

"Where are you going?" he shouted, his demanding tone raising the hackles of her spine.

"Upstairs," she replied coldly, keeping her back to him.

"I'll try to get home early," he said, his weary voice resigned, promising, attempting to console.

"Be my guest," Clea replied, stopping at the doorway, her hand resting on the arch to steady her trembling frame. "And if for some strange reason I'm not here when you return, I'll leave you a note. It'll be under the jar of iced tea in the kitchen cupboard. Don't forget to grab yourself a bite for dinner."

Forcing herself to climb the curved staircase, she heard the front door slam, Mitch's key turn in the lock. As silence descended over the empty house, tears welled up in her eyes, then spilled down her cheeks.

"Damn that man," she sobbed, wiping her faced with the hem of the oh-so-expensive peignoir.

Her quilt-covered bed looked more solitary than ever before. Clea slid under the crisp sheets and buried her face in the pillow. She hadn't even the energy to put on her street clothes and go out for a movie. Of course, she thought wryly, she could probably take in two shows and still be home before Mitch. So all she'd get for her endeavors would be a cold and four hours of tinsel boredom.

Clea was so involved in her thoughts that she didn't hear the key in the downstairs lock, didn't hear the footsteps on the stairs, didn't hear Mitch until he was standing beside the bed in the darkened room.

"I changed my mind," he said quietly, picking up the extension phone on the night table. Clea turned over, catching a glimpse of his suited figure in the shaft of silver moonlight that filtered in through the slightly parted drapes.

In low tones, Mitch was telling Rodriggs that he wouldn't be able to make it this evening. Something had come up and he would see him first thing in the morning. He certainly hoped the cost estimates would be revised to fit some semblance of reality, and he was also certain that the analyst could manage that reasonably well by himself.

There was a brief pause while he listened to the response, gave a slight nod, then added a genial, "Sorry to put you to any inconvenience, but it can't be helped."

The receiver went back into its cradle. "You win," Mitch said, taking off his jacket, tie, and shirt, folding them neatly, and placing them on a chair.

"You don't exactly lose," Clea replied, trying to sound lighthearted, wishing her nose wasn't quite so clogged from crying, wishing her face wasn't still wet from tears.

She watched Mitch take off his undershirt and slacks. His hard, lean body was first shadowed, then revealed in the moonlight, his muscles as taut as they'd been on their honeymoon. He removed his white jockey shorts, added them to the carefully arranged pile, slid under the covers, and put his warm hand on her bare shoulder.

"You're hard to resist when you set your mind to something," he commented softly, his fingertips trailing over her breast and then up to her still-damp cheeks.

Clea giggled. A most inappropriate giggle. She suddenly felt quite cheerful, as though she had won first prize in a contest where she'd thought she hadn't a chance. "What made you decide to come back?" she asked, smothering his face with grateful kisses.

"Temptation in lavender lace," Mitch quipped, obviously enjoying the onslaught of affection. "But remember, fair damsel, I did warn you that I was tired."

Clea smiled to herself, perversely thinking of Chapter 2 in the book concealed in her bureau drawer. "Well, my dear, you just relax. Clea Witherspoon Bottington will take care of everything."

Which she did. For a while. Until Mitch forgot how tired he was. He forgot almost everything except the hot, wet tongue in his ear, the soft mouth at the hollow of his throat, the nimble fingers that teased like gremlins along the short hairs of his chest, the hands that darted like demons down to his stiffening loins.

Driven by desire, Mitch started to shift position, but Clea didn't give him a chance. "I told you to relax," she whispered, her voice constricted by passion.

The nightgown of fine lace had long since been discarded, and suddenly Clea was an ivory odalisque above her husband, keeping pace with the urgent rhythms of his body. She moaned once, twice, and again as the sharp flames darted through her trembling body. And then she was silent and still, her swollen breasts pressed against his sweat-drenched chest, her face buried in the protective curve of his neck.

Mitch held her there, his powerful hands resting on her back, caressing the bare flesh no longer covered by the sheets or anything but his strong arms. "I guess I wasn't as tired as I thought," he admitted in a satisfied whisper.

"I guess you weren't," Clea purred, quite thoroughly content and hoping he wouldn't catch the note of triumph in her voice.

Eventually Mitch released her, flipped over on his side, and pulled the rumpled sheets around them. Clea snuggled into the warm curve of his body and kissed him lightly on the cheek. "Beats analyzing cost estimates with Rodriggs, doesn't it?" she teased, pushing back the waves of dark hair that had fallen forward onto his forehead.

It was fortunate that Mitch couldn't see the expression on her face, she thought, since he obviously had the illusion he was going to get some sleep. That this wasn't even a remote possibility was something she began to demonstrate the moment his eyes closed.

"Take it easy," Mitch protested drowsily as her hands began certain exploratory movements graphically described in the closing paragraphs of the book she had just studied. Tensing under her touch, he made an attempt at humor, saying, "The merchandise has just gone through the wringer and needs at least a few hours of slumber-pressing."

Clea insouciantly disregarded his pleas. "The merchandise will be pressed into perfect folds," she purred, erotically moving her fingers to where they would do the most good.

If Mitch had any further objections, he rapidly forgot them as his concentration was directed elsewhere. And this time, when he turned to her urgently, Clea let him have his way with her pliant, eager body, melting flesh blending into a soul-searing brew. Paragraph, chapter, and book were relegated to oblivion as Mitch cried out in need, Clea's responsive moans adding to the passionate symphony.

Mitch did get some, though not much, sleep, and no dinner. The gourmet shop delivery remained uneaten on the stove. And when he left for work the next morning, looking somewhat the worse for wear, Clea stretched luxuriously, yawned, and wriggled her toes under the covers. She supposed she should feel quite guilty. After all, her husband's mind needed to be razor-sharp for that contract analysis. But then, a good razor was a good razor and it's cutting edge could be honed by the merest touch of the sharpening mill. The truth of the matter was, she didn't feel guilty in the least. Quite the contrary; she felt better than she had in years—eight to be precise. The only item nagging at her conscience was the fact that it was already 9 A.M. and her novel was waiting.

3

PAGE 19, PAGE 20, PAGE 21. Clea's long fingers moved rat-a-tat-tat along the electric keyboard, hammering out word after word. Occasionally she arose, made another pot of coffee, paced the floor, stared out the window. In her designer jeans and pale blue angora sweater, wearing no lipstick and just a smidgen of pastel green eyeshadow, she looked like a teenager—but she certainly wasn't thinking like one.

Heroine Tanya had just thrown a stack of architectural sketches at her hero, Tony.

She was fed up with his know-it-all attitude, the way he leered at her as if she were just some scatterbrained skirt. Tanya was accustomed to having people defer to her judgment. But this man acted as if she had just graduated from grammar school with a degree in papier-mâché ducks.

29

Tony caught the sketches adroitly, rolled them up with deliberate slowness, and placed them on the butcherblock table next to him. It was the only item in their client's kitchen that wasn't piled high with building materials, materials chosen in deliberate disregard of Tanya's orders.

"Somebody should have taught you some manners by now," Tony snarled, his dark eyes revealing his contempt.

Tanya, furious beyond belief, told him to "stuff it." She had come up the hard way, born on the wrong side of town, and she knew how to handle a bully.

Only this bully didn't seem to know he was being handled. He moved so rapidly around the table, sinewy legs straining against tight faded jeans, that Tanya had no chance to reconnoiter. With a swift movement, his work-calloused hand grabbed her arm, pulling her toward him. "Maybe it's not too late to teach you how to behave," he said threateningly, forcing her against his rock-hard body.

"Leave me alone," she hissed, her fury increasing with each struggling movement.

"Not until you apologize," Tony said, his dark eyes embers about to ignite.

"I'll never apologize to you," she vowed, biting her lip to keep from crying out.

"Never is a long time," Tony replied assuredly. "And I've got nothing but time. Mr. and Mrs. Van Courtland won't be home until after five."

Clea was delighted. The sentences were flowing as from a pitcher of sheer sexual honey, and it seemed that nothing could stop them. Or so she thought until she had her hero and heroine locked in a passionate embrace on the Van Courtlands' living-room floor. Then she stopped typing. On the floor? Surely that would be uncomfortable.

Clea looked at the blank paper. She wanted realism, not make-believe. She got down on the apartment floor, wriggling against assorted pieces of furniture. The floor was predictably hard. How could anyone possibly enjoy herself while being pressed against such an unyielding surface?

Dusting her jeans off, she made a mental note to purchase a small vacuum cleaner for the apartment, then poured a final cup of coffee and concocted a tuna and egg sandwich. She thought of Mitch. She thought of their living-room carpet. And she smiled—just a slight tilting of the mouth which suggested a speculative anticipation.

The alarm clock beside her typewriter buzzed shrilly. With a start, Clea realized it was after three o'clock and she was due at the Museum Society fund-raising cocktail party at seven. Could she make it to the specialty lingerie shop and still get home in time to change her clothes for the reception?

Only if she rushed, she decided, and with that goal in mind she started to put the cover back on her typewriter. Then she stopped abruptly. Her novel, now moving along so well, still lacked a title. Jamming a fresh sheet of paper into the machine, Clea deliberated a moment. Titles were important, she knew, and should be carefully considered. But even a temporary one would suffice.

Still standing, she made a quick tap-tap on the keyboard. The words "Secret Diary of Delights" appeared in capital letters, and the page was added to the pile tucked away in the desk drawer. Humming a little tune about love in bloom, Clea felt quite satisfied with her day's labors. She felt even more satisfied as she contemplated her upcoming hurried shopping excursion and the night of "research" that would follow it.

"What do you have that's a wee bit kinky, but not over much?" Clea asked the saleslady less than half an hour later.

"What do you mean by 'not over much'?" the gray-haired woman replied. "We have many styles here, as you can see." She waved her hand at the plethora of undergarments on display.

Clea couldn't quite conceal her embarrassment. "Well, you see, my boyfriend insists on variety. And, well, he's a somewhat older man, and he shouldn't overdo it. So I want to please him, but I don't want to get him too excited. You understand, don't you?"

Thinking she probably sounded quite idiotic, Clea hesitated for a moment, but to her immense relief the saleslady was sympathetic. "We have many clients whose 'boyfriends' are mature gentlemen," she replied, "and I think I have the perfect item for your beau."

Clea's hazel eyes widened as they fastened on the burgundy wisps laid out carefully on the glass counter. Not only were the wisps practically transparent, but they also featured cut-outs in the most astounding places. Stubbornly resisting the urge to flee, she finally managed to stammer, "Haven't you got anything that's, uh, a little less naked?"

"Of course," the saleslady said matter-of-factly, her face registering only the slightest touch of amusement. Back to the drawer she went, again reappearing with burgundy, but this time in the form of a sheer baby-doll nightie with matching bikini string-tied bandana panties. "Will this do?" she inquired professionally. "It's quite a favorite with the older gentlemen. Or so I'm told."

"You don't wear such items yourself, I gather," Clea remarked, taking a fifty-dollar bill from her suede purse.

"Lord, no," the saleslady replied, looking aghast at the very thought. "Popsie and I have been married forty years, and I'd like to keep him around another forty, thank you. I wear flannels, head to toe. We already know what's underneath."

Despite her nervousness, Clea laughed. She was still chuckling as she left the shop, wondering if she could fit a similar saleslady into her novel. Ideas were popping into her head every moment now. It was amazing how interesting the world became when one had a definite project in which to engross oneself.

The purring Rolls Royce zigzagged easily through the rush-hour traffic, and she made it home by five o'clock on the dot. Kevin gave her a cheerful wave, then returned to an elaborate model train set, a gift from his doting grandmother. For a moment Clea marveled at how quickly he had grown from chubby toddler to lanky youth, then dismissed all traces of wistfulness to concentrate on dressing herself appropriately for the evening.

Entering her walk-in closet, which was the size of a small room, she rapidly surveyed the multiple rows of dresses covered with sheer plastic film, deciding finally on an electric-blue Dior, it's Grecian-style single shoulder hand-embroidered with gold filigree. Tossing it carelessly onto the bed, she studied herself in the dresser mirror, wondering how to conceal the fact that she hadn't had a moment to stop at the beauty salon. Although her hair was still clean, it certainly couldn't remain in this barrette-clasped ponytail. The women at the Museum Society came groomed to the hilt, and as Mitch Bottington's wife she'd be expected to outshine them all.

She gave the matter of her coiffure further consideration during her shower and had already settled the matter to her satisfaction when she emerged from the adjacent sauna to dry herself off with an immense monogrammed bath-sheet. Bending over, she gave her thick hair a few rapid brushstrokes, then wound the ash-blond strands into an elegant chignon. The style made her look rather sophisticated, she mused, and would provide the perfect framework for the diamond earrings Mitch had given her for their first anniversary.

Clea slipped the Dior over her head, then glanced at the slim Cartier watch on her wrist as she added the few remaining touches to her attire. Where was her husband? Usually he had Miss Hoven call when he was going to be late, but the maid had emphatically reported there'd been no messages.

As if in answer to her thoughts, the bedside telephone rang. "Hi, hon," Mitch said, his deep baritone sounding distinctly apologetic. "Something unexpected has turned up here at the office, and it looks as if I'm going to be a tiny bit late."

"Better late than never," Clea quipped, her light tone not quite matching the impatient tapping of her fingers on the nightstand. "But I certainly hope you intend to show up. The fund-raising is important to the museum. People in our position are expected to make at least a token appearance."

"Hmm," he said vaguely. Then his voice lowered as if he were afraid someone might be eavesdropping at his office keyhole. He cleared his throat. "As to last night, I'm afraid my behavior might have seemed somewhat...ah, unusual. You know, for 'people in our position.' If that's what you were referring to. But actually, though I didn't get a chance to mention it to you this morning, I do want to say it was, actually...a rather pleasant evening."

Rather pleasant? Clea's fair brows rose in disbelief. Was that the best her husband could come up with? Was he discussing a Disney movie? Well, come next round, replete with burgundy baby-dolls, he would certainly change his tune.

However, none of these thoughts were evident in her deliberately conciliatory reply. "So glad it suited you," she said in a warmly casual tone, just as casually adding that she did expect him to make it to the fundraiser even though she was sure they would both be bored to tears. "Perhaps it's just my mood," she added then. "I've had a rather long day, and it's definitely had its trying moments."

Mitch considered her days to be completely occupied with beauty salons, designer boutiques, and club meetings, now that Kevin was in school all day. Clea knew he wouldn't ask for details, and he didn't. "Long day here too, hon," he commiserated. "But save me a martini, because I definitely will make the cocktail party, if only to be seen as the escort of the most beautiful woman in the room." Clea's disposition lightened at the compliment, only to darken immediately as Mitch added, "By the way, tell Caroters I want to talk to him about the computer contract; he's not to leave before I get there."

Mitch considered all cocktail parties, opening nights, fund-raisers, and dinner engagements to be an extension of his business world. He usually dispensed the proper amount of hand-shaking and small talk, then closeted himself in a remote corner to talk high finance. It was Clea's job to add the decorative touch, make soothing sounds, and catch any gossip, important or unimportant, that might prove of value later on.

Like a team, she thought rebelliously, wondering why the concept, which had once pleased her, had suddenly grown so stale. "Like a team" she said out loud, a mental picture taking shape: Mitch as captain and his adoring wife as cheerleader . . .

No time to analyze her reactions now. It was already past seven. She waited until Mitch had finished explaining the essence of the computer contract before excusing herself with an "I've got to run before we're both late."

She thought it sounded somewhat abrupt, but Mitch didn't seem to mind. "If I didn't have you to uphold the

Bottington image," he joked, "the company would never have reached its present level of success. And I probably wouldn't have either."

Coming from her husband, that was quite a compliment, Clea thought. For some ridiculous reason, as she hung up the phone, she contrasted his behavior with her hero's. Tony would have made some snide remark, some derisive innuendo about Tanya being even later if he were around. How tacky. Mitch would never say anything like that.

On impulse Clea took the burgundy baby-doll nightie from the bureau drawer and held it up in front of her. She couldn't wait to see her husband's face when she put it on later that evening. Chances were quite good, she calculated with an impish grin, that after a few more nights of such costumes neither she nor Mitch would make it to any type of fund-raising event.

The thought that she was mixing up her novel with her private life flitted briefly across her mind. But then authors often got involved with their fictional characters, or so she'd heard. It was certainly no cause for alarm.

Flipping on the intercom, Clea paged their occasional chauffeur, who had been put on notice that he might be needed this evening. Then, removing her full-length mink coat from the closet, she dropped it across her shoulders, checking her image once again in the mirror. Hardly a Tanya, she mused, reviewing the regal reflection.

Abstractedly switching off the bedroom lights, Clea wondered what her feisty heroine would have done if her husband had insisted she go unescorted to a social function. Tanya would probably have gone to his office and sat there until he was ready to accompany her. What would someone like Mitch do then? It was a fascinating question to which Clea promised herself she would someday learn the answer. An answer based on her own personal research.

Still caught up in possibilities, Clea eased out of the limousine and briskly made her way up the marble museum stairs. Nodding to acquaintances, she shivered slightly in the damp night air, despite the enveloping warmth of her mink.

Spotting Caroters at the hors d'oeuvres table, she left her coat at the checkroom, then tried to wend her way deftly and inconspicuously to his side. The inconspicuous was impossible, as she should have known. Mrs. DomPeter caught her by the arm before she had even reached the halfway point.

"Darling, you look simply marvelous," the portly dowager gushed, her voice raspy from too many chain-smoked cigarettes and perhaps a tad too much imported bourbon. "You couldn't possibly be pregnant again, could you?"

If Clea had a touchy spot, this had to be it. But the years spent in finishing school learning to be a perfect lady "even if it kills you" plus the years spent as Mrs. Mitchell Eduard Bottington, stood her in good stead.

"Goodness, no," she returned, realizing she was using the same tone the lingerie saleslady had used to deny wearing peek-a-boo nighties to titillate her spouse. "At my age, one is certainly careful about those things. Besides, Kevin is enough. I don't see how I could handle another child."

"You never know until you've tried, dear," Mrs. DomPeter shot back, speaking from the perspective of one who'd avoided having any offspring at all. Her ménage consisted solely of five cats, all of which were declawed and neutered.

"Splendid reception, don't you think?" Clea cooed sweetly, deliberately changing the subject. "So many people managed to come, despite this terribly unseasonable weather."

"San Francisco is always unseasonable, my dear. And

speaking of people, where is your ever-so-handsome spouse? You always seem to arrive at these affairs alone. In my day, men accompanied their wives. Otherwise one wondered where they were, you know." There was a very perceptible pause before the smug disclaimer, "Not that Mitchell would do anything scandalous, of course. It just seems a pity he isn't around more. On the home scene, that is."

Clea gritted her teeth. The woman had never seemed more annoying or insensitive. Looking for a polite way to escape, Clea glanced around surreptitiously, then saw the perfect excuse. "Oh look there, Mrs. DomPeter. Glenda Moitran is here with her newest fiancé. Let's dash over and offer our congratulations before the crowd gets there."

Alerted to a splendid new opportunity for gossip, Mrs. DomPeter waddled off in the appointed direction, moving with as much speed as her matronly bulk allowed. Clea lagged increasingly further behind, then managed to effectively lose herself in the group surrounding the museum president.

The problem with being part of San Francisco's elite, she mused, was that everybody within that small circle managed to know everybody else's business. It was one of the reasons Mitch insisted that her behavior, and his, be above reproach at all times. But Mrs. DomPeter's malicious remarks had hit home anyhow. Mitch did spend more hours at Klectronics than he did with her. And while she understood that the company needed his guiding hand, there was no denying that—given state-of-the-art gossip—his long working hours did provide an opening wedge for the group's scandalmongers.

Squaring her exquisitely rounded shoulders and placing a professional Queen of England smile on her face, Clea remained at the fringes of the crowd that surrounded the museum president, then slipped away as soon as she caught sight of Caroters again. Heading in his direction, ever conscious of envious glances from those female guests who did not have her youthful figure or flawless complexion, Clea caught up with her quarry at the bar, ordering herself an Irish coffee as he ordered a martini.

"Mitch gave me direct orders to tell you not to leave until he got here," she said, looking appropriately apologetic before adding a conspiratorial smile. "He wants to chat with you about the computer contract and other technical minutiae."

Paul Caroters was a fairly short man, barely matching Clea's five feet six, but what he lacked in height he made up for in gallantry. "My beautiful Clea," he replied immediately, "as long as you stay here and delight me with your company, I'll wait for your lucky spouse until the sun comes up—which would, of course, offer not the slightest competition to your smile."

"Paul, you're wasting your time in the business world," Clea said, laughing. "If you took all your blarney and put it into print, you could earn a fine living as a poet."

"But I could only write poetry after gazing at you," Paul said, shrugging regretfully. "And, given your comfortable marital status to a man I much admire, I'm afraid my output would be severely limited."

As she stared at the whipped cream swirls melting in her steaming coffee, Clea felt the brandy's warmth remove the edge from her initial uneasiness at entering such a large party alone. She continued the idle chatter with a discreet return compliment and then inquired about Paul's rose garden, which she knew was his special pride and joy. Such a nice man, she reflected, her thoughts wandering a bit as he launched into a detailed description of a recent hybridization attempt.

Had she any right to expect her husband to make her feel like the most wonderful woman in the world? "Pleasant," he'd called their night of lovemaking. Caroters would never have used that word to describe such a passionate encounter. Not ever.

Clea was well into her second Irish coffee when Mitch finally made his entrance. She saw him over Caroter's shoulder, tall, very distinguished, and conspicuously handsome even among the many handsome men present. It seemed that everybody in the room made it a point to shake hands with him, including Mrs. DomPeter. She could see the woman babbling into Mitch's ear as he bent patiently forward. Then she glanced over at Clea and continued her monologue.

Clea's hazel eyes narrowed into slits as she observed the scene, an instinctive reaction that was immediately noted by Paul Caroters. He turned to follow her angry gaze.

"Very good-looking man, your husband," he commented, observing her face.

"I notice it whenever I get a chance to see him," Clea responded without thinking, a definite cutting edge to her voice.

"If I were fortunate enough to be married to someone as exquisite as you, I'd make it a point to have you see me as often as possible."

Realizing she had slipped in her impeccable role of "devoted spouse," Clea hastened to cover her error. "Paul," she gushed, "you've been a bachelor all your forty-five years, and you've had a long while to perfect your shameless flattery. But we both recognize that Mitch does the best he can, considering his work pressures. And of course whatever he does is done for the family. Which situation, by the way, I fully accept and appreciate."

Paul regarded her penetratingly, probably more than aware of the half-truth behind her words. But before he could comment, Mitch had joined them.

"Clea, you look lovely tonight," Mitch said, giving her an affectionate and socially appropriate peck on the cheek. She could smell his cologne; she could sense the warmth of his body through the custom-tailored blue suit. When all's said and done, she thought, her heart still gave a bounce whenever he entered a room. Only she did wish... Oh, what was the use? Mitch would never change. Barring some miracle, he would continue to be entwined in Klectronics' tentacles, just like his father before him.

Patiently she listened to the technical conversation that buzzed about her. The men were so engrossed in check-lists and balances that they seemed to have forgotten she was there. By virtue of long practice, Clea managed to appear raptly attentive, but her daydreams soon took her elsewhere—into the land of Tanya and Tony. She wondered what sensuous predicament to enmesh them in next.

She envisioned Tony stripped to the waist, his burly chest covered with a mat of wiry brown curls; pictured his rock-hewn legs encased in tighter-than-tight denims, which emphasized rather than concealed his superb male anatomy. He was barefoot. He was doing... what? Cooking dinner—that was it. Masculine men always seemed extremely sexy puttering around in kitchens. She recalled the time Mitch had invited her to his room for dinner a few weeks after they met. Keeping herself under control that night had taken all the strength she could muster. She still remembered the knots in her stomach when she returned to the dormitory. Heroine Tanya would have those knots too, but what excuse could Clea find for bringing her to Tony's apartment at all?

Various possibilities occupied her mind for a while, but as the hour wore on, Clea's thoughts drifted to the sheer baby-doll nightie with its equally sheer bikinis. It was amazing what using one's imagination could do for the libido, she thought, grinning to herself.

Maybe she should be totally direct and don her gauzy

attire in the bedroom. Or should she be a little more circumspect and approach Mitch in the living room? She could insist he have a nightcap with her before turning in, and then she could race upstairs and change... That would be preferable, she decided, if they were going to try making love on the floor. If she started seducing her husband in the bedroom suite, it would be difficult to explain why they were eschewing the comfortably padded king-sized mattress in favor of the wooden floor, its punishing surface softened only slightly by the amber wool carpet Clea had chosen years earlier.

Clea was so immersed in detailing this scenario that she almost missed Mitch's comment, which was addressed to her for a change. "Paul wants to go for a cup of coffee after the reception," he said. "Someplace where it's not so crowded. Are you still awake enough to come with us? I know you've had a busy day; it's fine with me if you'd rather go home."

Clea could see her carefully laid plans going kerplunk; a fistful of stardust dumped into stew. If Mitch went with Paul, he wouldn't get home until 2 P.M., and then he'd hit the bed like a bag of flour. This she knew from past experience. While her mind was running on fast-forward, she managed to appear as if she were seriously considering the offer. Which she was not. All Clea could think of was all that plotting and shopping she'd done—and all for nothing. She felt like screaming. Right here in front of all these elegantly clad scions of San Francisco society.

Click-click-click. Bingo! Clea turned, not to Mitch, but to Paul Caroters. She opened her hazel eyes as wide as possible. Her demeanor was as innocent, as much like that of a guileless waif as her high-cheekboned, classically contoured face would permit. And then she said, her voice low and conspiratorial, "Paul, before Mitch arrived, you commented on how seldom I get a chance to be alone with my good-looking husband . . ."

Of course Paul hadn't actually said this; Clea had. But she was hoping with all her might that Paul's innate sense of chivalry would force him to go along with her minor fib. For a moment she held her breath. Mitch was glaring at her as if she were totally addled, and Clea began to fantasize about disappearing into her empty Irish coffee glass like the genie she suddenly wished she was.

She needn't have worried. Paul, romantic to the core, came through beautifully. "Your gorgeous wife is absolutely correct," he said gallantly. "Except she's only telling half the story. I also joked that if I was married to someone as exquisite as she, there would be no question of where I spent my evenings. No offense, Mitch. Just a lonely old bachelor casting wishful pebbles in the stream."

Mitch seemed to be having trouble controlling his temper as he glanced from one to the other in an effort to figure out just what was going on. But before he could respond, Paul painted the finishing touches with deft verbal brushstrokes.

"Mitch, I'll give you a call at the office tomorrow. I think we've managed to accomplish enough for tonight. And your lonesome wife does seem to want you all to herself. I think we'd better oblige her."

Before Mitch could protest, which he was clearly about to do, Paul shook his hand, nodded a "good evening" to Clea, and drifted off into the crowd. Mitch, who had remained immobile during the entire exchange, gradually let the twitches of repressed anger show in his normally composed mien.

"I know that was quite dreadful of me, darling," Clea soothed apologetically, placing her hand on Mitch's muscular arm and gazing dove-eyed into his stormy face. "It's just that I'd much rather snuggle up in the car with you than study the folds of the chauffeur's cap. Besides, your folds are much nicer, and so are your delicious nooks and crannies." The latter was said in such an obviously sultry manner that Mitch almost looked over his broad shoulder to see if anyone nearby had overheard.

"What on earth has gotten into you?" he growled angrily.

"You did dear, remember?" Clea raised her long lashes, looked down demurely, and then up again, reviewing her spouse with obvious erotic invitation.

"That has absolutely nothing to do with right now," Mitch snarled, his gray eyes hard as steel under his thick dark brows. "You know how I feel about the Bottington image. Which isn't the least bit enhanced by your implication that you're being ignored by your heartless husband. Who, by the way, was merely trying to complete some necessary business."

"Confiding in an old friend like Paul Caroters is almost like talking to a priest," Clea contested hotly, wondering why Mitch was making such a fuss. "Paul won't breathe a word of this to anyone. It's not as if I'd announced my intentions over the museum loudspeaker."

"That's another item we have to discuss. Later," he added sharply. Mitch was clearly disinclined to do battle in front of the hordes of gossip columnists present, and when he realized his taut shoulders and bunched fists might be attracting unwanted attention, he rapidly brought himself under control.

"Do occupy yourself for a bit, my dear," he said glacially, his hooded falcon's eyes glinting with a fury that only Clea could see, while his sensual mouth softened into the smile he chose for public view. "I've got to make a few more obligatory social rounds before we leave."

Clea, who rarely displayed any signs of temper, managed to control an impending eruption with a barely noticeable tightening of her patrician jaw. "Of course, my

dear," she retorted, her compliant tone discernibly arti-
ficial. "I also must do my social duty. How selfish of
me to remain here with you and Paul. Why don't we
meet in half an hour? That should be sufficient, don't
you think?"

Watching Mitch's tall, well-built form disappear into
the crowd, Clea had a spiteful desire to replace the burgundy baby-dolls with a porcupine coat and necklace of
garlic for bedwear that evening, short-sheeting the bed
while she was at it. But that wouldn't do much for her
novel, she thought wryly.

Head held high, expression completely serene, Clea
did exactly what Mitch expected of her: she circulated.
Making the usual inane remarks about the weather, she
moved on to such topics as the success of the fund-raising
drive, the need to have some more brochures printed,
the white-elephant sale the museum would be sponsoring
next month.

But with every single sweetly smiling remark she made,
her blood continued its slow simmer. She was not accustomed to being so bluntly put in her place. Mitch
might be a Bottington, but *she* was a Witherspoon. She
certainly needed no lessons in social etiquette from him.

At precisely the half hour, Clea got her mink from
the checkroom, tossed it around her slim shoulders like
a royal robe, then meandered regally over to Mitch, who
was in the midst of addressing one of the museum trust-
ees. "You did say you had an early business meeting
tomorrow, darling," she purred, her voice dripping honey.

The distinguished gentleman immediately offered his
apologies for keeping Clea's husband so long. Thus,
Mitch had no excuse to prolong the conversation. But
his gray eyes were icy agates when he and Clea finally
reached the marble museum stairs, and the muscle twitch-
ing in his cheek foreboded trouble ahead.

Mitch slid into the low-slung black leather seat of

their Ferrari, opening the door for Clea without a word. Maybe she had pushed things too far, she thought, reviewing her actions. Burying her hands in the folds of her mink so Mitch wouldn't see how they were trembling, she tried desperately to think of something to say.

Mitch, however, was at no loss for words. "Okay, out with it," he said brusquely as the engine purred into action. "Eight years of absolutely satisfactory agreement on our respective social roles and all of a sudden not one, but two different people start telling me that I leave you alone too much. I'd like to think it was mere coincidence, but somehow I don't."

Clea shot him a quizzical glance, which Mitch returned with an inquisitor's impatient glare. "I haven't the foggiest idea of what you mean," she finally managed to blurt.

"Don't you?" he said caustically.

"Not in the least," she snapped.

"When I came into the foyer, that busybody Mrs. DomPeter managed to trap me long enough to comment that my exquisite wife certainly appeared forlorn. That it was none of her business, of course, but could it be that "poor Clea's" unhappiness was due to my overwhelming devotion to Klectronics? In the same gin-soaked breath she managed to tell me that her own dear departed spouse had managed to get all his work done and still make it home for dinner once in a while too."

She knew she shouldn't, but the mere mention of mousy little Chauncey DomPeter made Clea burst into spontaneous laughter. "That witch's husband was never home a minute more than he had to be. In fact, it's been suggested that he had his heart attack so he wouldn't have to come home at all."

Mitch shot her a warning look, but it wasn't quite so harsh as it had been a moment ago. Clea began to relax and deliberately snuggled up against him. Glad for a chance to change the subject, she used the opportunity to give her husband a playful kiss on the cheek.

"Will you swear to me that you had nothing to do with it?" he queried, keeping his eyes glued to the road ahead but beginning to sound less angry.

"Mr. DomPeter's heart attack or his wife's nosy remark?" she teased, placing a hand on his hard muscled thigh.

"Clea." Mitch sighed, covering her slim hand with his larger one. "Don't play games. This evening has been trying enough as it is."

If you knew what games I have planned for you later, Clea thought mirthfully, you'd throw me out of the car. Relieved, she kissed his cheek again. With considerable zest, and truthfully enough, she replied, "On my honor as a Bottington, I had absolutely nothing to do with either problem."

This seemed to end their argument and the conversation shifted to the exchange of juicy tidbits each had picked up at the reception. Clea assumed Mitch had forgotten their whole disagreement. But he wasn't quite ready to let the matter drop.

"No more interference in business," he warned as they entered the discreetly luxurious Hampstead Estates. A mere flick of a hidden button triggered the remote control on the iron-barred gates of their winding driveway.

"The master orders and I obey," Clea acquiesced, attempting to sound as obedient as possible. However, her mind, freed from the burden of Mitch's wrath, was now whirling back to her original scheme. It's lucky men don't understand how women think, she mused, or they wouldn't have us around at all.

The house was warm and quiet, with Kevin and the servants all sleeping soundly. Did she dare to proceed with her plan? She could leave matters to rest for a while, try the floor routine tomorrow perhaps, or even next week. But she wasn't quite sure where her wandering spouse would be tomorrow or next week. His out-of-town sojourns were often planned mere minutes in advance, and she really shouldn't pass up the present opportunity.

It was not a difficult decision. "To atone for my interfering behavior," Clea said demurely, "let me make you a nightcap, darling. It will help you unwind and make me feel better too."

Mitch seemed about to refuse, but Clea looked so woebegone and contrite that he apparently had second thoughts. Reluctantly, he agreed.

Clea poured him a double shot of bourbon, maneuvered him over to the velvet couch, and then excused herself to "slip into something more comfortable."

Her slow and even pacing continued until she was out of eyeshot, at which time she took the stairs two at a time. Her electric-blue Dior with the gold filigree was tossed hit-or-miss onto a chair, and nylons and undergarments were dumped unceremoniously in the wicker hamper. Moving at lightning speed, she donned the burgundy baby-doll nightie and managed to get the pantyties into a loose bow.

Released from its pins, her ash-blond hair tumbled around her face in unrestrained waves. Clea gave herself a quick but thorough review in the vanity mirror before augmenting her flimsy attire with a generous dab of expensive perfume. The revealing nightie made her look like a harem girl out to seduce a reluctant sheik, she concluded, smiling to herself as she realized that fantasy wasn't too far from the truth.

Mitch was still sipping his bourbon when she reappeared. No appropriate opening lines occurred to her, so she simply decided to be forthright, to act as though this were just a typical cozy evening at home and that nothing out of the ordinary was going on.

"I wanted to show you my new pajamas before you got so relaxed you went to sleep," she began, making a gliding, long-legged entrance into the living room.

Mitch raised one dark eyebrow at the apparition in scant burgundy, and the man who was seldom overtly astonished by anything appeared completely at a loss. "What did you put into this drink?" he finally blurted. "Because either I'm hallucinating, or you're trying to catch pneumonia."

If you think you're hallucinating now, Clea thought triumphantly, noting that his glance was riveted exactly where she wanted it to be, I wonder what you're going to think half an hour from now? But she didn't say that. Instead she said coquettishly, "I haven't the slightest intention of catching pneumonia with my handsome husband in the room. Super outfit, don't you agree?" Her words were accompanied by a seductive pirouette, well calculated to show off all her best features.

Mitch was about to begin blushing again. He was doing his best to maintain his control, but with nine years observation experience Clea could easily recognize the symptoms. His gray eyes were still fixed on the wanton display in burgundy, but soon they dropped and traveled slowly upward all the way from bare toes to gleaming mass of hair, then down again, even more attentively. Clea smiled. Her husband might be staid, but he was a male and also very human.

"So this is why you wanted me home early," he murmured huskily, putting his unfinished drink on the adjacent end table. She gave him no chance to lead her toward the bedroom. Moving swiftly to the couch, she parked herself deliberately on his lap.

"Aren't you going to stop me from catching cold?" she purred provocatively, teasing the hollow of his throat with light fingertips as her other hand played with the hair at the back of his neck.

Mitch would have had to be superhuman to resist her, she figured, and was gratified when he didn't even try. Spurred on by his obvious response, Clea next unbuttoned his white shirt and pressed her full breasts against his chest, at the same time nibbling on his earlobe. It was a technique acquired in a research chapter titled "How to Arouse a Man," and it was certainly proving quite effective.

"Let's go upstairs before I can't walk," Mitch finally pleaded after a soul-searching kiss in which darting quicksilver tongues left scalding trails of liquid fire in their wake. His pupils were dilated with a desire that matched the need now so urgent in Clea's own body. She had to fight to prevent herself from agreeing. Agreeing to anything.

"I can't make it that far," she moaned, with more truth than she might have expected. "Mitch, I want you. Now." The insistency of her statement was enhanced by her fumbling fingers, which moved to his belt buckle and then to the mat of hair on his tense abdominal muscles, where, barely able to restrain her passion, she kneaded his sinewy flesh.

Not quite sure what was happening to him, and apparently in no mood to protest, Mitch was putty in Clea's now eager and supremely nimble hands. When most of his clothing had been deftly removed, she wriggled off the couch just long enough to dim the living-room lights. Returning to her husband she took his hands in hers and pulled him off the couch. Getting him to the carpet was easy, the shortest of distances, and Mitch knelt over her, his need so great it could barely be contained.

Clea's nails tore into the well-defined ridges of his sinewy back as his searching mouth moved over her face, her neck, the swollen nipples of her breasts, the seductive curve of her stomach.

And then the room ceased to exist. They were on the

moon, on Mars, on some far-off galaxy showered by exploding meteors. Clea heard Mitch moan "I love you," and then nothing else at all except a rapturous cry which seemed to emanate not from their entwined bodies, but from some point eons away in endless space.

When they returned to their senses, the room was silent as a cathedral. Mitch held her tightly, rocking her in his strong arms, cradling her forehead against his damp chest. For some inexplicable reason, Clea felt salty tears in her eyes. She wondered where they came from and why they were there. She had the feeling someone had just given her a gift, tinsel-wrapped and infinitely precious. And it was only much later, the next morning after her husband had left for work, that she even remembered her original reason for wearing the diaphanous nightie, or why she'd opted to make love on the floor.

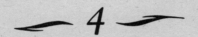

IN THE DAYS that followed, Clea did not return to her
apartment sanctuary. First there were some meetings to
which she had committed herself months ago. Then there
was a day-long fitting with her dressmaker. There were
two home dinner parties in a row for out-of-town guests
who, because of their dealings with Klectronics, had to
be wined and sumptuously dined at the Bottington estate.

Mitch seemed somewhat abstracted, often glancing at
her in a rather quizzical way when he thought she wasn't
looking. He made no mention of the unusual lovemaking
session or its unorthodox site. This hardly surprised Clea,
who was well acquainted with his reticence when it came
to private matters. But he was also unusually quiet, even
for a normally quiet man.

Absorbed in her own hectic schedule, Clea passed all
this off as mere preoccupation with business. However,
when she came across him at home one afternoon, pack-

ing his suitcase, she immediately and inexplicably became both annoyed and frightened.

"Where are you going?" she asked, watching him pack shoes, shorts, shirts, and toiletries in his customarily methodical pattern.

"Milwaukee. There's a problem with one of our distributors, and it has to be dealt with immediately. I'd send somebody else, but it's such a mess that I'd eventually end up having to do it myself anyway. So I might as well go and do it right in the first place."

"It's freezing in Milwaukee this time of year," Clea objected pettishly. "And you've got subordinates who are very well paid to do the troubleshooting. Why can't you let them try?"

She knew the answer before her husband voiced it: because his subordinates were competent, but in this case couldn't know all the intricacies of the situation; because there was a time factor in the distribution process, and this matter was urgent; and because, he repeated, he wanted to do it right in the first place. Typical Mitch. Take the world on his shoulders and never complain about the Atlas load.

Clea watched him remove a suit and winter coat from the closet and carefully lay them out on the bed. She continued her silent observation as he took some notebooks from his leather briefcase and replaced them with others.

"How long will you be gone?" she asked after a long silence.

"Maybe a couple of days, maybe a week. Depends on how long it takes," Mitch replied abruptly. Apparently she had interrupted his concentration with her petty resentments about his departure.

Clea was more than resentful. As far as she could tell, the trip was totally unnecessary. Mitch was going because he wanted to go. What other reason could there possibly be? And so she made a request she had never even considered before. "Take me with you," she said.

Mitch barely looked up from his packing. "No," he said curtly.

"Why not?"

"Because . . ." he began, then hesitated before continuing deliberately. "Because you're needed here. You've got the house to take care of. You have to be around in case Kevin becomes ill. You have a dozen and one things to do. And in Milwaukee you'd have nothing to do, and I wouldn't be free to entertain you, and—"

"And maybe I'd get in your way," Clea said sarcastically, finishing his sentence for him.

"That's not what I was going to say."

"Isn't it? I mean, I'd really be a nuisance, wouldn't I? Tagging along at your heels like a puppy. Saying the wrong things. Asking for a few minutes of personal time from the ruler of an electronics empire who really can't be bothered with such trivia. Why don't you just admit it?"

Mitch slammed the suitcase shut. "I haven't got time to argue," he said. "When I return, Clea, you and I are going to have a serious talk. Your whole attitude has changed lately. All of a sudden there are ridiculous nightgowns, personal comments made in totally inappropriate social settings, and now this senseless desire to accompany me on a business trip where you would have nothing to occupy you at all."

Fury burned through Clea's marrow. The finishing-school graduate, the submissive wife, the impeccably mannered socialite vanished; and in her place was a shrill harridan, the painful words *ridiculous, inappropriate,* and *senseless* shredding the last remnants of her self-control.

"I know why you don't want me to come with you," she shrieked, making no attempt to modulate her tone.

"Do you?" Mitch replied, his face a granite mask, his eyes glaciers.

Clea stopped screaming. Her hazel eyes narrowed and her voice became triumphantly analytical. "You're afraid," she said bitingly.

"I'm not afraid of anything," Mitch shot back, his voice low, controlled, threatening.

"Yes, you are. You're afraid if we're alone together for a week you'll get to know me too well. You're afraid that you might not like the reality behind your 'perfect' wife. And you're afraid that I'll put on another of those *ridiculous* nighties and make you lose control again."

Mitch turned his back on her and stared at the damask bedroom curtains as though mesmerized by their intricate pleats. Eventually he asked in a much softer tone, but still not turning around, "Clea, what do you want? I hate to see the two of us hurting each other like this. We mean too much to each other. Tell me what it is you want. I'll try to give it to you."

Shame coursed through Clea. What right had she to rail at him like a fishwife? This was the man who had fathered her son, who had always made certain she had the best of everything. He had never once tried to restrict her lifestyle, had never denied her anything. Was it his fault she was bored and lonely? Or was it her own?

"Please take me with you," she said, going up behind him and putting her arms around his waist. "Please. I won't be a bother to you."

Mitch swiveled around, tilted her chin up with his large, gentle hand, and searched her pleading face. "Not this time, Clea. I would if I could, but for various reasons, I can't. Next time I will. Promise." He kissed her softly on the lips and pulled her tightly against him, cradling her in his arms as if she were a sorrowful child.

"Then come to bed with me now," Clea murmured, nestling against him like a baby bird, wanting desperately to delay his departure. Every time Mitch traveled, she was afraid she'd never see him again. That the plane would crash, that he would be involved in an auto accident, that some horrible thing would happen and he would disappear from her life forever. She never told him of these fears—it would have served no purpose—but they tugged at her heartstrings each time she bid him a casual "See you whenever" farewell.

"I've got to catch the four o'clock flight," Mitch replied, drawing slightly away, kissing her forehead, and running his fingers through her now disheveled hair.

"You can catch a later flight," Clea cajoled. "What difference does it make, really? Either way, you'll arrive too late to get any real work done. And it would make such a difference to me if you stayed just a while longer. Please."

Mitch sighed. She could sense, almost see, the inward struggle between conflicting demands. And then he capitulated.

"Okay. If there's a later flight, I'll take it. But don't ever tell anybody the reason, because I'll deny it to the last."

He went to the telephone book, checked the number, dialed the travel agency, and told them there had been an unexpected business complication. Could they arrange a later flight? He nodded, made a few pencil scratches on a pad of paper, and, saying "Thank you," hung up. "All arranged," he remarked, toying with the pencil as if it were a foreign object.

"Do you want to play cards while you're waiting?" Clea bantered, a wellspring of happiness bubbling inside her.

Mitch put the pencil down with deliberate slowness, and a muscle twitched in his cheek as he said warningly, "Clea, don't you dare..."

"You don't want to play cards?" she questioned, pretending astonishment. "Not even gin rummy or a little solitaire? My goodness, Mitch, what on earth has come over you?"

"You little minx," he replied hoarsely, striding over to pick her up in his arms. "I didn't postpone my trip to play solitaire, and by the time I'm through with you, you won't have the strength to pick up a card."

"Listen to the caveman," Clea taunted with a silvery laugh, her arms wrapped comfortably around his neck. "There I am, going about my job of plucking grass for our dinosaur, and you come along threatening to subdue me with a club."

"That's a good enough analogy." Mitch gave a satisfied chuckle as he placed her none too gently on the bed. He began to unbutton his shirt.

"You don't want me to put on one of my ridiculous nightgowns?" Clea smiled, kicking off her shoes. "It just so happens I have one that resembles a leopard-skin loin-cloth."

"You wouldn't be wearing it for long anyhow," Mitch replied, removing his tailored slacks and uncharacteristically letting them drop to the floor. "Why go to all that bother for nothing?"

Clea reviewed her naked husband in the light that filtered through the damask curtains. It had been a long while since she had seen his naked body during daylight hours, except for brief snatches in the morning as he dressed for work.

Mitch had a fantastic physique. His arms were well muscled, with a sprinkling of dark hairs on the upper part, a curly layer of it on his forearms. His chest was powerfully hewn, the mat of hair thicker here, forming a triangle that narrowed to a point below his waist, then repeated itself in protective fashion around his loins. His hips were slim and his legs long and firm, matching his arms in texture.

"You're a very, very beautiful man," Clea whispered huskily, feeling almost hypnotized.

"I'll feel even more appreciated when you've got your clothes off," Mitch suggested lazily, standing above her like a vanquishing gladiator.

"You take them off," Clea challenged, her expression more than a trifle wicked. "If you can, that is."

Mitch could and did. In fact, Clea offered very little resistance to his disrobing efforts. But this time it was her staid husband who was doing the seducing.

"Over on your tummy," he directed affably, "and I'll rub your back."

Clea flipped over, allowing herself to relax under the firm ministrations of his facile fingers. Mitch kneaded her muscles, beginning at her neck and then moving down along her shoulder blades, her spine, the curvaceous indentations of her waist. She purred softly, her pliant flesh like putty beneath the gentle touch of a giant. His hands moved to her alabaster buttocks, drifted lightly into the crevice between, then down to her thighs, caressing her private recesses so lightly she wasn't sure if it was accidental or not.

When he finished with her toes, he murmured, "Turn over, my lovely," and proceeded in the same erotic downward pattern, stroking her breasts, her abdomen, her hips, the curling tuft of blond hair that covered the warmth inside, the slim length of her calves.

"Feel better?" he asked huskily, giving her a light, affectionate kiss, then just a slightly longer one which enticed but did not torment.

"One hundred percent better," Clea whispered adoringly, reaching up to play with the mat of tempting hair on his brawny chest, her fingers seductively grazing his erect nipples.

"I hope I didn't put you to sleep," he added with a slight smile that reflected her own.

"Not at all," Clea replied, her gaze melting into his so that they seemed joined at the very essence of being. "In fact, I was just thinking that one good turn deserves another. So why don't you flip over on your tummy and let your devoted wife here give you some very pleasant memories to carry along with you on your trip."

Mitch did as he was told, and Clea exactly as she'd promised. But where her husband's massage had been instinctive and therapeutic, hers was slightly more calculating and erotic. There was a particular technique she had studied in one of her "how-to" reference books, and this seemed as good a time as any to try it out. Maybe Mitch wouldn't like it. Then again, maybe he would.

He did. Very much. And he had been in Milwaukee two full days before he finally thought to wonder where his sheltered wife had obtained such an extensive fund of carnal knowledge.

Mitch was gone a week. To Clea's continuing amazement, he called every evening. She made it a point to be home then, as well as in the mornings to send Kevin off to school and in the afternoons to welcome him home. All other waking hours were spent cloistered in her secluded apartment, the typewriter drawing her there like a magnet.

The characters in her novel had taken on a life of their own. They did what they wanted to do without much effort on Clea's part, and a steady flow of descriptive words quickly filled the seemingly endless sheets of white paper. Tony and Tanya seemed to be overcoming their initial conflicts, and Tanya, despite some continuing reservations, was finding the construction supervisor increasingly appealing—regardless of his male supremacist tendencies.

Tony, in turn, had actually become more cordial, allaying her suspicions that he was "only out for what he could get." In her newly relaxed frame of mind, Tanya acceded to his suggestion that he come to her condominium to review some details of the rewiring plan.

When he arrived, having telephoned to say he would be a bit later than the appointed time, Tanya had already begun efficiently to tackle another project. His knock at the door at 9 P.M. found her with stacks of drawings piled up beside the dining table, a frown of concentration on her face.

"You look tired," Tony commented sympathetically.

"This arboretum within an arboretum is so complicated, I don't know why I started it tonight," Tanya replied, her voice hoarse with fatigue.

"Tell you what. How about we postpone our professional negotiations for a few minutes, and I'll give you a neck rub that I learned to do during my high school football days."

It sounded marvelous, in fact as well as in print. Clea's adroit hero not only unknotted the muscles in the heroine's neck, he also unknotted a goodly portion of her resistance. Clea completed Chapter 5 as if some wordsmith were dictating the scenario, sentence after sentence flying from her brain to her dashing fingers. It was only late that Friday afternoon, as the week drew to a close and she reviewed her work, that she marveled at her newly acquired ability to conjure up such accurate descriptions of passionate lovemaking.

However, as she got ready to pick Mitch up at the airport, it occurred to Clea that her fantasy muse was hardly a product of chance. After all, she had actually lived each sensuous episode herself. She was only describing a reality that promised to become even more vivid with the passage of time and continued experimentation on her part, with her husband a willing, if not quite cognizant, ally.

Mitch's plane was late and, as usual, Clea fretted, asking the gate attendant a series of inane questions which helped only momentarily to soothe her anxieties. When the flight finally arrived, two hours behind schedule due to adverse weather conditions, Clea kept her gaze fixed on the exit door. She was clad comfortably in her flattering white sweater, kick-pleat tartan wool skirt, and low-heeled black leather pumps.

It seemed her husband was the last one off the plane. Clea's face lit up in a smile of relief, which lasted only until she saw he was not alone.

"This is Sonora Cameron, purchasing manager for our Milwaukee branch," Mitch said by way of introduction, giving Clea a socially self-conscious kiss. "She's thinking of transferring out here, and I said she could stay with us for a couple of days while she reviewed the San Francisco Klectronics setup. I expect we'll have an opening here in the near future."

Sonora was almost as tall as Mitch. She had high cheekbones, slanted green eyes, a dusky complexion, and jet-black hair styled in a casual blunt-cut that barely touched her shoulders. She looked extremely cool and efficient, from her perfectly tailored gray jacket and matching skirt to her low-heeled slate shoes. Her handshake was equally cool, as was her low, perfectly modulated voice.

"I hope this won't put you to too much bother, Mrs. Bottington. You husband was kind enough to offer hospitality when he saw I was serious about this."

Clea did mind. Especially since Mitch hadn't even bothered to call her and ask whether this would interfere with their personal plans. After all, her home wasn't a hotel (the appropriate place, she privately thought, for Miss Cameron—presumably "Miss" as she lacked any wedding band—to stay).

However, Clea was careful not to let her hostility

show. "It would be my pleasure to have you as our guest for a few days," she responded courteously. After all, what was done was done, and it was her job, as the wife of Mitchell Bottington, president of Klectronics, to be a gracious hostess. Even though she felt like taking out her checkbook and telling her unwelcome visitor that she would gladly pay her hotel bill.

She continued to stew in silence as they waited for the baggage. It wasn't only that Clea objected to the arrival of an unexpected houseguest, *per se.* Sonora's stay would interfere with her writing schedule. It would also interfere with the rather intriguing bathroom scene she had planned for this evening to remind Mitch of joys not available when he traveled. That is, she thought with a covert glance at Sonora, joys she assumed were not available when he traveled. For the first time in her married life, Clea had the nagging suspicion that she might be taking a lot for granted.

That Sonora Cameron was definitely single she learned on the ride home. The Klectronics purchasing manager was twenty-seven years old, had started out as a secretary, taken night courses in management and finance, and eventually obtained a master's degree.

"It wasn't easy," said Sonora, more than a touch of self-satisfaction in her crisp voice. "But it's been worth all the hours of effort, not only mentally but fiscally as well. My job is fascinating, Klectronics pays me well, and your husband is one of the few upper-echelon men who give more than lip service to the idea that women are of value in corporate hierarchy."

There was no real rationale for Clea's mounting annoyance. Or so she told herself as she reheated the dinner left by the cook, adding enough lettuce to stretch two portions of salad into three. Nevertheless, as she sat at the dining table, her simmering irritation reached the boiling point. The conversation flowing around her centered on technical matters of which she understood very little. Mitch didn't seem in the least inclined to seek a private moment of reunion with her. In fact, as the hours passed and the discussion moved on to the living room, her husband's interest in Sonora's opinions seemed to intensify rather than decrease.

It was close to midnight when Clea finally excused herself, pleading fatigue. "Please don't interrupt your conversation because of me," she said smoothly, the "me" coming out slightly more emphatically than she had planned.

Her farewell smile to Sonora was as cordial as she could make it, but her parting contemplation of Mitch certainly was not. Whether he recognized the hurricane warnings in her hazel eyes or was actually feeling fatigued himself, he rose reluctantly.

"I know tomorrow's Saturday," he said, addressing Sonora, "but if you'd like a quick preview of our main office, I could show it to you in the morning."

"If it isn't any bother to you or your wife," Sonora replied appreciatively, "I would love to do exactly that."

"Oh, Clea won't mind," Mitch stated with assurance. "Will you, dear?"

"Not in the least," Clea snapped, exhaustion removing the last remnants of her patience. "After all, you've been gone a whole week. What's another day?"

The waspish remark seemed to bounce right off Sonora, but it wasn't lost on Mitch. Clea sensed his tension and knew there would be an argument, one that she was far too tired to cope with right now.

Mitch didn't slam the bedroom behind him, but he might as well have. "Sonora Cameron is one of the brightest young executives Klectronics has," he rebuked Clea acidly. "She took over a department that was consistently in the red, made some personnel adjustments, and for the first time in ages that department is now turning a profit. We're extremely fortunate to have her working for us. I assure you, she's had many other good job offers. So would you please mind your manners while she's here? You've been like an ice cube all evening long, and that parting comment was totally unnecessary."

Clea didn't answer. She went into the bathroom and put the new plush two-person bath towels back into the cupboard. She put away the Jacuzzi scintillating bubble-making attachment she had purchased that morning. She hid the rose-scented massage oil guaranteed to promote instant lust. Then she came out, pulled a seldom-used persimmon flannel nightgown from a drawer, and locked herself back in the bathroom to change.

When she emerged, Mitch was already in bed, the lights off. She climbed in next to him and put a tentative hand on his bare shoulder.

"I'm sorry, Mitch," she said apologetically. "I guess I was just looking forward to our being alone."

At first she thought he hadn't heard her. But then, as he pulled the blankets up to cover his shoulder, he replied in an almost remote voice, as if talking more to himself than to her. "Maybe you should find something more intellectual than shopping to occupy your spare time," he said drowsily. And with that, he fell asleep.

Clea curled up at the opposite side of the bed, hot tears burning at her eyelids. She did have something intellectual to do with her time. She was writing a book. And it was turning out to be a rather good book, too. As an author, even an unpublished one, she was pursuing a goal. One that wasn't easy. One that took time, and concentration, and called for continued learning. She was hardly the dumb bunny Mitch apparently thought she was. It was a long time before she fell asleep.

She was still thinking about it the following morning. And although she had to devote a great deal of energy to planning that evening's entertainment—an impromptu but elegant welcoming cocktail party Mitch had tersely instructed her to arrange in honor of Sonora Cameron— her thoughts kept returning to her secret writing.

Maybe it would be in her best interest after all to confess that she was writing a novel. She didn't have to say what kind. She could merely imply that she had begun it during his absence, that she had been researching it for quite some time, and that it had a romantic theme.

The more Clea thought about it, the better she liked the idea. With Mitch in the know, she wouldn't have to sneak away in the afternoons; there'd be no need to tell any more fibs about her whereabouts. She could write at home. Besides, establishing herself as something other than an empty-headed socialite would put her on a conversational par with her competent houseguest. At least it would give her something to talk about, since problems with dressmakers and the household staff were obviously of no interest to someone like Sonora Cameron.

As she put the finishing touches to the buffet table, arranging the pink baby roses and bright yellow daisies in an attractive pattern among the surrounding ferns, Clea grew more and more positive that she was on the right track. She would tell Mitch after the cocktail party, when she would somehow manage to get him alone. Better yet, she would tell him in bed. There at least she would have his full attention, away from Sonora's endless technical blather.

That evening Clea felt positively buoyant as her guests arrived. She circulated almost merrily, accepting compliment after compliment on the steaming trays of food, the platters of iced Gulf shrimp, the tiny caviar hors d'oeuvres. Her custom-made dress, a yellow chiffon of the same sunny hue as the daisies that graced the table, swirled just below her knees and flattered her youthful figure. As the evening progressed with supreme smoothness, Clea felt confident that Sonora, in her stark black sheath, couldn't possibly hold a candle to her.

Nor could her uninvited visitor compete with Kevin, who was informing everyone within earshot that, "This is my Daddy," then going up and standing next to Mitch to demonstrate the resemblance.

Initially Clea tried to convince him to scoot off to bed and his favorite TV program, but Mitch put a protective hand on the boy's shoulder and said, "It doesn't bother me. In fact, I kind of like it. He's such a great kid." This was said with a proud, fatherly smile and was all the encouragement Kevin needed. He was Mitch's shadow until the party ended slightly before midnight.

Once her son was safely under the covers, having fallen asleep even as his father carried him upstairs, Clea flopped onto the living-room couch. Kicking off her yellow shoes in relief, she listened for Mitch's return, sure that everything would soon be perfect in her orderly world. Even Sonora's presence didn't disturb her, although Clea couldn't help comparing her guest's fresh face to her own wilted countenance.

The speech was prepared. Clea had been rehearsing it mentally all evening as she listened with one ear only to the torpid cocktail party conversation that hummed around her. "Darling," she would begin, "I've had the most fantastic idea..."

Mitch would listen attentively, fascinated by every syllable. Clea would build it up, savoring the anticipation, yet not revealing her secret. Then, just as Mitch was about to burst with curiosity, she would say in dulcet tones, "Darling, I've had second thoughts; this is far too personal. Forgive me, Sonora, but I'd better discuss it with my husband privately." This would be accompanied by an insouciant shrug of the shoulder in the direction of the upstairs bedroom.

As her husband strode into the room, his athlete's springing grace not at all diminished by a full day's work plus the evening's rigors, Clea rose for full effect. "Darling," she began, "I've had the most—"

"Before you tell me about the new gown you bought," Mitch interrupted, rubbing the back of his neck and grinning with smug satisfaction, "let me clue you in on what happened this afternoon."

"But darling," Clea protested, eager to get on with her speech.

"I promise you'll have my undivided attention in a minute. But first let me tell you that I've accepted the interim presidency of the Parent-Teacher Liaison Group at the Country Day School."

"But they're tearing each other to shreds over this ban-the-book thing," Clea sputtered in shock.

"Certainly," Mitch said coolly. "That's why the prior president quit. He couldn't stand the heat. The P.T.L.G. knows they can count on me."

"Count on you for what?" Clea asked with some trepidation, sensing the answer before it came.

"To protect the untainted minds of children," Mitch replied firmly. "Plus, of course, those of the parents. No one wants that sexually titilating swill cluttering up his household bookshelves."

"Mitchell, you're being entirely too narrow-minded," Clea objected, her confession now the furthest thing from her mind. "The books in question are quite harmless, a far cry from pornography. Many are by our most literate authors; others make fine diversionary reading. What harm can they possibly do?"

"It's the principle of the thing," Mitch retorted, equally stubborn.

"Perhaps your wife might feel better if she thought of your candidacy as a superb public-relations gambit. It could be most helpful to Klectronics," Sonora interjected in her ever-competent, corporate manner.

"Precisely," Mitch said, looking quite pleased that at least one other person in the room had instantly grasped his point of view.

"Promoting the image of Klectronics is not a good reason to promote censorship," Clea snapped, wishing Sonora would mind her own business. "Besides, you can't tell me that neither of you has ever picked up a novel that had a few erotic passages." The statement was pointedly aimed at her spouse, whom she knew thoroughly enjoyed spy thrillers with seamy overtones.

Sonora looked as if she would never consider perusing anything but a book on advance accounting procedures, and Mitch's craggy mien turned instantly stony. "That's quite beside the point," he stated firmly. "We're adults. But even so, we should be the first to admit there's entirely too much smut around these days."

The silence in the room was like a vacuum, with both Sonora and Mitch making a determined show of studying their crystal brandy snifters.

Clea's mind jumped to what she considered the best scene in her novel. Tanya was attending a homebuilders' conference and had decided to take a quick shower in her hotel room before proceeding to the afternoon seminar. Since she was expecting a female colleague to drop off some literature, she had left the door slightly ajar.

"I'll be finished in a minute," Tanya called out, observing a shadow in front of the shower enclosure.

"Take your time," responded an amused baritone. "I've got all day."

"How did you get in here?" Tanya said, her voice uncharacteristically high pitched.

"You left the door open for me, so I walked in," Tony responded with assurance.

"Well, it's still open, and you can just walk right

out," Tanya commanded, trying to sound as sure of herself as the sight of her defenseless naked body would allow.

"Not until I talk to you," Tony stated calmly.

"You can take a running jump off a short pier," Tanya shrieked, the sound muted by the shower's din.

"I'd just as soon get wet with you," Tony countered.

What followed was pure, unadulterated "smut," if sex in a shower must be considered that. Mitch would surely think so. But Clea didn't. What was a little erotic adventure between two consenting adults? Her scene was drawn quite beautifully, with more erotic innuendo than clinical detail.

"I don't agree with you," Clea said abruptly, breaking the deadly quiet that hung like a pall over the living room.

"You don't agree with me about what?" Mitch queried, his tone that of a man accustomed to instant and respectful accord.

"About one person having the right to decide what another person should read or write," Clea said haughtily.

Mitch shrugged, pushing back a lock of dark hair that had fallen onto his forehead. "You're entitled to your opinion," he said coolly, his tone of voice making it quite clear that he didn't believe that at all. "However, since I do intend to be interim president of the Parent-Teacher Liaison Group and to run for the school board after that, and since I do intend to take the conservative side on this issue, I'd suggest that you, as my wife, keep your opinions to yourself. Until the election is over, anyway."

"I will never admit to a soul that you read steamy spy thrillers," Clea said, thoroughly riled. "And I'll try to refrain from embarrassing you by admitting that I occasionally enliven my solitary evenings with a bit of romantic fiction."

Her allusion to lonely evenings was apparently the final straw. "The problem, perhaps, lies with your inability to distinguish between romance and pornography," Mitch snarled caustically, totally ignoring Sonora's obvious interest in what should have been a private family feud.

"The problem, perhaps, isn't mine," Clea shot back. As far as she was concerned, it was her parting remark for the evening. Pivoting rapidly on her stiletto heels, she walked huffily out of the room.

But the dialogue continued in her mind long after she pretended sleep on the farthest corner of their king-sized bed. She had no intention of abandoning her novel, especially now. Tanya and Tony were at the stage where sexual attraction gave way to true romance, even though neither of them was quite ready to admit it.

"I've got it!" Clea suddenly said out loud, her words having no effect on her husband's soft, even breathing. She looked at him with a wicked smile on her face. You can catch more flies with honey than with vinegar, she mused.

Cuddling up against him, she unbuttoned his pajama top and ran her long fingers deftly and lightly over the dark mat of hair that covered his muscular chest. When that failed to awaken him, she repeated the procedure, this time adding soft ministrations with her mouth along his warm flesh.

"For goodness sake, Clea," Mitch mumbled drowsily. "Not now. It must be after two o'clock."

Clea's response was to run the pointed tip of her pink tongue along the outer part of his ear. You can go to blazes, she thought perversely, the ramrod virility pressing against her thigh ample evidence that Mitch was responding, despite his husky protestations.

"Damn you," Mitch rasped, his large hands moving eagerly over her firm breasts, thumbs caressing the aureolas until her nipples stood erect.

Clea arched against him, her alabaster silkiness a dancing flame in the darkness, her darting tongue teasing and tormenting him even as his roaming hands brought a burning liquid lava to her loins.

She felt herself melting, dwindling into nothingness, moving from one fathomless delight to another in endless waves that crested, then rose again. Her skin was part of his skin, moist and alive. His legs were her legs, his mouth, her mouth; there was no difference. As Mitch's flickering tongue sought her most secret crevices, the symphony that flowed between them reached a crescendo and Clea had only one fleeting reverie before she acquiesced completely to his hammering need, a need that perfectly matched her own.

It was a reverie that faded quickly, to resurface the next morning. She stood outside the shower listening to Mitch humming happily under the stinging spray, then slowly opened the enclosure door. "You're going to have a difficult time distinguishing between romance and pornography, my dear mule of a husband," she whispered under her breath as she joined him under the steamy waterfall.

She told herself she was only checking on the accuracy of the chapter she had written. And it so happened, as she and Mitch finally emerged, breathless, from the shower stall, she knew she was going to have to rewrite a few paragraphs. The interlude under the pelting water had revealed that there was considerable need for editing, and by the time Mitch returned with Sonora later that afternoon, Clea had an even more devilish idea in mind. All in the interests of research, of course.

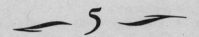

5

"SONORA, DARLING, HOW glad I am to see you," Clea exclaimed effusively as her guest and husband sauntered through the door.

It was difficult to determine whether Sonora's or Mitch's dark brows rose further in astonishment. Up until that minute, Clea's attitude had been one of impeccable, if icy, politeness, so her sudden turnabout was viewed with obvious skepticism. A skepticism Clea chose to ignore.

Kissing Sonora affectionately on the cheek, Clea took her by the hand and then clutched Mitch's hand, impatiently pulling them down the long entry hallway. Mitch's hand was like wood, and Clea giggled inwardly as she watched Sonora struggle to keep her composure.

Her giggle notwithstanding, Clea was deadly serious. She had only one goal in mind: to get rid of Sonora Cameron. The purchasing manager had not only interfered with her writing schedule, but she so reinforced Mitch's businesslike, Klectronics spirit that she posed a real threat to Clea's marriage-renewal project. There was no denying it: Sonora was a bad influence on Mitch. Clea smiled. She'd had a brainstorm, a true burst of genius. One that would further her research aims and at the same time would rid her of this dangerous pest.

"I could barely wait for you to get home to ask you about a marvelous idea I had," Clea said excitedly. "Of course, it isn't entirely my own idea. You inspired me, Sonora. I can't tell you how grateful I am."

From the corner of her eye, she could see Mitch loosening his tie with his free hand, a sure sign that he was becoming uncomfortable.

"Clea, are you going to let us in on this 'idea' of yours," he said slowly, "or are you just going to give us clues and make us guess?" Clea sensed that he wanted to tell her to shut up, and that only Sonora's presence was keeping him from doing so.

"Oh, let's discuss it after dinner," she demurred. "And speaking of dinner, I have another surprise for you. I hope you'll like it."

By this time they had reached the living room and Mitch had managed to disengage his hand and reach for the scotch in one smooth motion. Sonora awkwardly backed away, mumbling something about powdering her nose. When she returned moments later, she stationed herself as far from her hostess as possible—unless, that is, she wanted to open the bay window and jump out. So far, so good, Clea thought.

"Do tell us your surprise," Sonora requested, attempting to lighten her steel-edged voice with only minimal success. She looked, Clea mused, almost like Mitch in her gray business suit, white blouse, and low-heeled black shoes. The only difference was the crisply folded burgundy bow at her collar in lieu of the standard man's tie.

"Well, let me show you," Clea said, smiling. "Just follow me."

Leading the way toward the dining room, she paused outside the double doors with her hand on the crystal knob.

"Ready?" She paused. Mitch looked as if he could willingly strangle her. Sonora's expression was definitely uneasy.

Clea opened the door slightly and called through the marginal space, "Are you ready?"

"Ready, Mommy," came the return cry, followed by what sounded like a cricket's chorus of giggles.

"Here we go," Clea said, swinging the doors open wide. With a small, pleased smile, she took in Sonora's gasp of astonishment, the slow rosy glow of embarrassment creeping up under Mitch's collar.

She had told Kevin to use his imagination in preparing dinner, and the seven-year-old had eagerly complied. The dining room lay before them, balloons tied to each chair and to anything else that string could be wound around. Miniscule shreds of paper, obviously meant to simulate confetti, lay in jumbled polka dots on the plush ecru carpet.

On the table was a paper cloth decorated with squirrels enjoying an alfresco tea party. Champagne glasses held tiny bouquets of smashed dandelions; and an enormous candle, dredged up from heaven knows where, occupied center stage, along with three party hats saved from last New Year's Eve.

"Do you like it, Daddy?" Kevin asked with happy anticipation. "I wanted to do something special for you when you came back, but I didn't know what."

"I see," Mitch said, with a sidewise glance at Clea

that clearly announced they would discuss this at length later. Yet, to his credit, he strode into the room without missing a beat, picked up Kevin, and perched him triumphantly on one broad shoulder.

"It's fantastic," Mitch praised, reviewing the scene, as though he were about to award it four gold stars. "A touch of genius," he added for good measure. "I'll bet Mommy gave you lots of help."

"Oh, no," Kevin said, wiggling to be put down. Then he stood up straight as possible, cherubically confronting his father's six-foot frame. "Mommy said I could do it all by myself. Even the dinner."

Sonora's gasp was barely audible. Mitch didn't hear it. He was busy staring at the two seven-year-olds emerging from the adjacent kitchen, both draped in black crepe paper clearly meant to simulate waiters' tuxedos.

"This is David and this is Boppo," Kevin said, bubbling over with boyish enthusiasm.

David nonchalantly wiped his nose with the back of his hand and then walked briskly over to a damask-covered chair, pulled it out, and, turning to Sonora, announced, "You sit here, ma'am." Given a lack of alternative, Clea's guest did as instructed.

Boppo held the chair for Clea.

Mitch helped himself with apparent gusto to the mostly uncut lettuce leaves that filled a large salad bowl in combination with some large chunks of carrot which the children, in their exuberance, ignorance, or perhaps both, had forgotten to peel.

Kevin chattered away, explaining to his daddy in great detail how Mommy had taken him to the supermarket and let him choose the ingredients for tonight's meal. "At first I didn't think I would know how," he admitted, "but Mommy said I had very good judgment, and she knew you'd be pleased. You are pleased, aren't you, Daddy?"

"Absolutely," Mitch assented, piling a second helping of salad onto his squirrel-festooned paper plate. Clea felt a sudden surge of fondness for her husband.

"David," she requested, "perhaps Miss Cameron is shy about taking another serving. Would you be so kind as to help her?"

David complied, with another sniffle.

The meal proceeded with only such minor mishaps as Boppo tripping over his own feet and spilling a glass of water on the carpet, the hot dogs being somewhat over-cooked, and the frozen hot dog buns being a trifle un-derthawed.

Through it all, Clea maintained an expression of in-nocence that would have qualified her for an angel's portrait, and Kevin kept up a steady stream of conver-sation. Mitch ate three hot dogs smothered with mustard, plus a large helping of lukewarm, soggy french fries. He did all this with a smile on his face, further confirming Clea's conclusion that she truly adored him.

"Mitch," she said casually, "I must say that when Kevin proposed this meal, I hoped it would be as much a treat for Sonora as for you. I wanted your guest to have the chance to sample a genuine family meal."

Mitch said nothing and Clea raced on. "I wanted to make you welcome, Sonora. Partly, I admit, because of another idea I've had. The one I mentioned when you came in earlier, remember?"

Mitch shrugged. Clea liked the way his chest moved when he shrugged. Very rugged, she thought.

"You said something about inspiration," Mitch of-fered cautiously.

"Exactly," said Clea brightly, turning her attention to her guest.

"I wanted Sonora to get the flavor of my family-oriented life," she continued, "because I would like to get the flavor of her business-oriented life. At Klectron-ics."

Mitch looked perplexed and Sonora looked wary, but Clea went on with her speech. "My husband recently suggested that I develop my intellect," she explained. "So I thought perhaps it would help if I got to know you and your work better, Sonora, since Mitch so admires your professionalism."

"Sonora is one of our best employees," Mitch inter-jected, to Clea's carefully concealed delight. The word *employee* was a perfect reminder of her place in the scheme of things.

"What do you propose, Mrs. Bottington?" Sonora asked.

"Clea," Clea corrected with friendly firmness. "I pro-pose that for the next day, or two, or three, I inconspic-uously tag along with you as you review the Klectronics operation here. I promise I won't get underfoot."

Sonora turned to Mitch as if looking for a polite way out of the situation. However, she didn't get much succor from her host, who was avidly digging into a plate of chocolate syrup that was theoretically just an overlay for the dab of vanilla ice cream underneath, but which ac-tually dominated the plate. David was offering jelly doughnuts to accompany the dessert.

"Is there any particular reason you want to do this?" Mitch asked between spoonfuls.

"I told you, darling. I want to sharpen my intellect. I want to understand you better."

As Clea spoke there was a crash of glass from the kitchen. Kevin ran in the direction of the sound, with Mitch following a few steps behind when his wife seemed disinclined to move. "Do what you want," he said over his shoulder.

Clea and Sonora stared at each other across the table. Then Clea lifted her lukewarm glass of overly sweetened lemonade and proposed a toast. "May we spend many hours together," she said, her tone as sugary as the drink.

Sonora had no choice but to follow suit, and Mitch, peeking into the dining room to make certain all was well, seemed quite pleased to witness this moment of accord between his wife and his guest.

The next day as Clea literally dogged Sonora's heels through the corridors of the Klectronics plant, she quickly became aware of a special language being spoken by the employees, plus a special unspoken pattern of communication.

The line workers wore white smocks and, in some instances, safety glasses. But in the business offices, both men and women were quite smartly dressed. Clea had never really been "behind the scenes" before, and found everything faster paced and more highly charged than she had imagined.

Glad that she'd decided to wear her dark blue French wool suit with the peach silk blouse that set off her flawless complexion, Clea noted that Sonora had switched to dark brown, a hue that did nothing to flatter her dusky complexion; but the severity of its cut added a certain touch of class, which Clea duly noted in the tiny, much-scribbled-in pad that never left her hand.

Throughout the afternoon she researched potential dialogue for her novel, paying special attention to any scenario that could be transferred to the offices of either Tanya or Tony.

By 5 P.M. she still hadn't seen Mitch, nor had she let Sonora out of her sight. The unwelcome houseguest had by now developed a slight twitch in her right eye, which got worse as Clea asked her thousandth question of the day.

"Surely you must be somewhat bored by now," Sonora said, giving her a hopeful look.

"Not at all," Clea assured her. "I can't wait to get home to ask you more questions. It's all quite fascinating to a sheltered housewife like myself. And it's not often that I have a houseguest who proves so cooperative."

For some reason—perhaps it was the prospect of another Kevin-catered dinner—Sonora suddenly looked off into space and said something about taking a room closer to the plant.

"I hope I haven't made you uncomfortable in any way," Clea exclaimed.

"Not at all," Sonora denied, imitating Clea's tone. "You've been a most devoted hostess. It's just that . . ."

"You'd rather be closer to the plant," Clea said, finishing the sentence for her.

"Precisely," Sonora stated in her clipped voice. "In fact, I was thinking of making the move as soon as we finish here. I hope your husband won't mind."

"Oh, I'll take care of Mitch," Clea said. "He and I can always spend the evening reviewing what I've learned today."

"No doubt," Sonora stated, not quite concealing her skepticism about her hostess's ability to absorb such complex corporate material.

Clea merely smiled. It was a smile that deepened as Sonora strode away, not even turning around for fear of encouraging Clea to follow. But Clea had no intention of wasting any more time at Klectronics. She had come up with a scintillating idea for a new bedroom scene, and she couldn't wait to see, feel, and enjoy Mitch's reaction to this one. The curtain would go up as soon as Kevin was safely tucked into bed.

Mitch was late in returning home. When she'd received no message by 8 P.M., Clea stopped pacing long enough to dial his office. The only response was a recorded announcement stating that Klectronics was closed for the day, followed by the request that she "Please leave a message following the bleep."

Knowing her husband sometimes ignored his phone at night to avoid distraction, Clea called the security division. The guard told her he had seen Mr. Bottington about an hour earlier, but not since.

While it wasn't unusual for Mitch to be late, it was unusual for him not to phone, and Clea's worry deepened as the grandfather clock struck the hour of nine.

"How come you look so grumpy?" a pajama-clad Kevin asked, tearing himself away from the television set for a final peanut butter and jelly sandwich before bed.

"I'm not grumpy," Clea replied. "I'm just wondering where your father is."

"Oh, he probably found something interesting to do at work."

"Don't you think there's anything interesting to do around here?" Clea inquired acerbically.

Kevin shrugged and then focused his full attention on his mother, who was still wearing the blue business suit. "You look like that man-lady who was staying here," he observed bluntly.

Since that was precisely Clea's intention, she nodded affirmatively. "This is considered de rigueur corporate attire," she informed him.

"Is that the same as rigor mortis?" Kevin asked, licking the last of the peanut butter off his fingers.

"You had better get to sleep before I decide you watch too many detective shows," Clea stated firmly. Reluctantly, Kevin allowed her a kiss on the cheek, then padded off to his room.

Clea looked at the clock again, then into the mirror beside it. Her ash-blond hair was pulled severely back into a braided bun, and her makeup was a little heavier than usual, but still quite discreet. She adjusted the high collar on her peach silk blouse, dusted invisible specks from her dark blue wool jacket, and debated once again whether to add a dark blue silk bow around her neck. This time the bow won, as did the very expensive Dior eyeglasses she had once purchased on a whim but never worn.

The effect, she decided, was more than corporate; it was almost professorial. Clea walked into the living room again, and reaching under a couch cushion, she took out a pocketbook whose cover depicted a pirate passionately mashing a semiclad female against a ship's mast, and began to read.

"Goodness," she thought as the clock struck ten. "To get into *that* position, a person would have to be double-jointed." But then again, maybe not. She made a mental note to check it out that very evening. That is, assuming her errant spouse ever showed up.

As if in answer to her musings, she heard Mitch's car pull into the driveway and a few seconds later the sound of the garage door opening.

Clea hastily stuffed her reading material back into its hiding place, then picked up a bulky tome entitled *Surviving in the Corporate Jungle* and buried her nose in it.

"Didn't think you'd still be up," Mitch said by way of greeting. "Where's Sonora?"

Clea wanted to say that a touch of her magic wand had converted their houseguest back to her true self—a computer. Instead, she casually replied that Sonora had insisted on moving to lodgings closer to the plant. "I told her how sorry we'd be to lose her," Clea stated, shading the truth a bit. "I've so enjoyed talking to her. But she still insisted on leaving."

"Just as well," Mitch said wearily. "Even though Sonora's tremendous company, I don't feel like talking to anyone right now."

That was fine with Clea, who was in no mood for conversation herself. During her long day she had mentally compared Mitch to every man she'd met at Klectronics, which, considering the number of engineers employed there, was a rather goodly number. Beyond a doubt, she'd decided, her husband was the most handsome and the most masculine of the lot. In fact, right now, in the privacy of their living room, he looked extremely enticing. Clea licked her lips in anticipation of the activities ahead, but Mitch's thoughts were clearly elsewhere.

"I ended up spending two entire hours with a self-appointed committee from the Parent-Teacher Liaison Group," he said irritably.

Uh-oh, thought Clea. "Oh, I bet you're exhausted, you poor dear," she said sympathetically. "Is that what kept you so late?" If she didn't handle the next few moments properly, her evening's plans would be ruined.

"Yes. They wanted me to add a facts-of-life primer for kindergarten students to the approved reading list."

"Well, it seems a bit early to me," Clea stated, "but in today's world maybe basic reproductive knowledge is necessary, even for very young children."

"Klectronics president Mitchell Bottington recommends teaching five-year-olds all about sex," Mitch said, proclaiming the anticipated newspaper headlines.

"Aren't you exaggerating slightly?" Clea queried.

"I wish I were," Mitch retorted, running his fingers through his dark hair, disarranging it enough to give him a tousled, almost boyish air that Clea found even more appealing than his corporate look. Forward and onward, she mused.

"I wonder what the P.T.L.G. antismut committee would say about this book," she murmured, holding up the thick volume on corporate survival techniques she had placed on the coffee table.

"I haven't had a chance to read that one yet," Mitch said wearily, taking off his suit jacket, removing his tie, and opening the top button of his white shirt.

Clea's hazel eyes glimmered, and she was rather pleased she had opted for the glasses. It wasn't wise at this point to appear too eager. She'd have to lead up to this gradually.

"Well, Chapter Six tells how to deal with male-female liaisons, which, to quote, 'have a tendency to occur in the executive boardroom after the other employees have left for the day.'"

"If I ever catch anybody doing that at Klectronics, they'll be looking for another place to work," Mitch stated somewhat primly.

Clea fought back her desire to unbutton the rest of his shirt for him, just to be helpful. Instead she commented, "Well, severely tailored business attire can actually be quite provocative on some women."

"I disagree," Mitch responded flatly.

"Why?" Clea asked, rising from the couch, walking over to him, and letting her peach-polished fingertips rest ever so lightly on his shoulders.

"I have other things to do besides spend valuable time determining whether or not a female staff member is dressed provocatively," Mitch averred.

"You mean you don't find the thought of removing a business suit, piece by inviolate piece, rather exciting?" Clea asked, letting her fingers drift slowly down his muscular arm to form a caressing cup around his elbow.

"I don't think I've ever given the matter a moment's thought," Mitch stated, a slight frown knotting his dark brows. Clea reached up to erase it, then let her index finger waft delicately over his nose and around the outlines of his mouth.

"Could it be if I asked you to remove my business suit piece by piece, you would refuse?" Why were men so obtuse? Did her executive spouse need to be hit over the head with a hammer? Perhaps so.

"I did notice you're still wearing that nice suit you

brought back from Paris last year," Mitch said, as the trailing of her hand over his firm abdomen finally brought a speculative gleam to his dark-lashed gray eyes.

"You're catching on," Clea said with amused patience. "Would you like to proceed to lesson two, which is removing these useless glasses?"

Mitch complied, kissing her lowered eyelids upon completion of the assigned task. With a sideways glance, Clea saw the carelessly discarded glasses land directly over the spot where her "pirate" romance was concealed. For some reason the thought pleased her immensely.

"This bow tie around my neck is rather uncomfortable," she said suggestively.

"Far be it from me to let you suffer so," Mitch commented, warming to the game. Clea sighed rapturously as his hand slid far below the area covered by the neck bow. But she forced herself to hide her response, replacing the dreamy-eyed expression with a stern look.

"You're supposed to remove my plain, starched shirt first," she said. "That's corporate boardroom step number three."

Mitch took his time, unbuttoning the blouse with delicious care. "You're certain this is in the book?" he asked somewhat huskily, his mouth moving to the crevice between Clea's breasts.

"Absolutely, positively," she replied with equal huskiness.

Mitch's tongue had begun to make exploratory forays around her ear. Placing a hand on his arm, Clea stopped him before her lacy brassiere ceased to become a restraint.

"You're not doing this properly," she chided, her own passions threatening to overwhelm her.

"I have every intention of being improper," Mitch said salaciously, sucking at the very tip of her earlobe. The resulting sensation traveled clear down to Clea's toes, making them curl of their own accord.

"According to page one hundred and thirty-six, paragraph three," Clea instructed, trying to keep as straight a face as possible, "the male employee carefully removes the now unbuttoned blouse from the female employee and just as carefully folds it over the back of an executive boardroom chair. This is just in case she has an appointment for a business dinner at the Emu Club afterward, and must appear with her clothing properly pleated."

"Oh," said Mitch, the laugh lines at the corners of his eyes deepening. He drew back in an attempt to look properly businesslike, but the effect was definitely negated by the unseemly bulge that did little for his trouser pleats. Clea pretended to ignore it.

"You're supposed to be taking off my blouse," Clea reminded him.

Mitch did as he was told, albeit slowly, his strong hands trailing gently across her creamy shoulders, softer than silk as they made lazy circles over the golden down at the base of her neck. Then, gently, they unfastened the one remaining hook on her wispy brassiere.

Her husband was becoming quite an erotic artisan, Clea reflected appreciatively as she watched him fold the pale peach blouse, ever so neatly, and place it on a living-room chair. At this moment, Mitch looked almost as he had the night they'd first met. On that occasion they had gone to a small coffee shop near campus, one of those places with checkered tablecloths and drippy candles stuck in Chianti bottles.

There had been a red carnation in a simulated-crystal vase, and Mitch had removed it, presenting it to her as if it were a rare orchid from a faraway continent. Clea, in accepting it, had felt her heart stop, felt the world stop. She had taken a mental photograph, and now the memory reemerged of its own accord from deep within her heart and mind.

She had stuck the carnation into her upswept hairdo, instantly changing her image from sophisticate to hoyden. And all the while her eyes had never left Mitchell Bottington's face.

He had been very tan then, but that was the only real difference. Nothing else seemed to have changed. The shirt was still white, even though it was now button-down Oxford instead of sporty turtleneck. The shoulders were as broad as ever under the fabric, muscles rippling easily as he made his way back across the room. Long legs, still in navy tailored slacks, still moving with grey-hound grace. And his eyes, the color of smoke, of evening fog, of mockingbird wings...

"You're staring," Mitch said gruffly, abruptly turning on the bone-melting grin that Clea had seen so rarely in the past few years.

"Have I told you recently that I love you very much?" she asked with intense seriousness.

"Not really," Mitch replied, his mouth curving into a teasing smile. "In fact, in recent weeks you've been unpleasantly argumentative. That is, when you're fully dressed. Out of your clothes, I must admit, you've been extraordinarily affectionate."

"Well, I love you very much," Clea responded, her tone daring him to refute the declaration. "Nevertheless," she continued, not about to be sidetracked from her project, "we can't allow that to get in our way. Let me remove your shirt."

Her teasing fingers making diversionary forays from each tiny buttonhole, Clea at last worked the shirt from her husband's powerful frame. Clad now in form-fitting white T-shirt, Mitch pretended boredom, a pose he couldn't maintain for long. As his breath grew quicker, Clea slipped her fingers under the taut white cotton and began drawing lazy circles across his chest.

"Are you certain that's what comes next?" Mitch asked,

a catch in his voice, as Clea began toying with the curling mat above his belt buckle.

Pausing briefly, Clea feigned puzzlement. "Well, perhaps you should take off my skirt before I do anything else. Or are you supposed to remove my see-through camisole?"

Mitch did both, in the order mentioned, in a matter of seconds. He then, very precisely, folded both on top of the pale peach blouse.

"You know, I find I do enjoy removing a business suit, piece by piece," he observed, giving her full, unfettered breasts and slim waist a thorough review.

"Me, too." Clea laughed, making a clumsy return attempt at pulling off his T-shirt. Eventually Mitch helped her with the task, but only after she promised to fold it very neatly. In case he had to go to the Emu Club afterward for a corporate dinner meeting.

The room light now outlined the sharply hewn musculature of his chest, back, and arms. Black hair curled tantalizingly over his pectorals, tapered down to his rib cage, and then narrowed even further to the point of a V as it approached the waistband of his slacks.

"What's next, teacher?" he asked, his thumbs moving slowly over the firmness of her pink aureolas, stroking them gently.

"I forgot," gasped the recipient of his caresses, as a curling, licking flame seared her loins into open fire.

"I hope you're not on the payroll of this corporation," Mitch teased, slipping his hands down to the silk-covered roundness of her buttocks at the same time that his searching mouth moved to take possession of her eager, succulent lips.

Toying with her tongue, he at first refused to permit its exploration of his own mouth. When he relented, heeding Clea's whisper-soft moans, he expertly guided the pink tip inward, reveling in its sensual assault on his palate.

Clea could no longer fight her descent into molten oblivion. Her fingers fumbled with the clasp on his black leather belt, sought the warmth of his body even as she began to unhook and unzipper. Suddenly she felt Mitch move back a step.

"Clea." Her own name seemed to come from far away.

When the name was repeated, insistently, she looked up, a slight flicker of fear in her opalescent eyes.

There was something in the craggy lines of her husband's face that she had seen before, but she couldn't remember quite when. No, that wasn't true. She could remember. She had to remember. Instinctively she knew that his withdrawal had a deep significance.

"Clea, do you believe there is a difference between pornography and romance?"

"Of course," she replied, her hands resting on the wiry blanket of dark curls that covered his chest, seeking succor there, awaiting instructions on whether or not to move on.

"What is it, then?" Mitch persisted, kissing the top of her head gently, as if to show that the question was meant kindly.

"Well . . . it's the difference between sex and love," she responded, a slight frown spreading across her face. She gazed up at him. That wasn't a very good answer. Surely she wasn't thinking clearly, or she could come up with a much better one. Sex and love—at least when it came to Mitch—were inseparable in her mind. But then, as abruptly as the sun emerges on a not-quite-spring day, Mitch smiled.

"You must think I'm out of my mind," he commented, pulling her almost roughly toward him, lifting her slight frame just far enough from the floor that her stocking-covered feet barely grazed the plush carpet.

"Well, I wasn't exactly expecting a philosophical discussion right now," Clea murmured, her voice muffled in the heated hollow of his neck. "If that's what you mean."

"It's a problem with us Bottingtons," Mitch said, frowning, his hands now on her tiny waist and lifting her upward until her head was slightly higher than his own. "We're perhaps too serious..."

Still puzzled, Clea glanced down. The tight expression had not left his face. Again she tried to place that look. Again she failed.

"Clea." His voice was soft, his eyes troubled as he lowered her back down to the ground.

"What, dearest?" she whispered.

"This...this isn't Bottingtonlike behavior," he told her, flushing slightly. "I'm beginning to wonder..."

"Come here," Clea purred, pulling out the pins that held her hair in a restraining chignon, letting the ash-blond curls tumble wantonly around her shoulders. She leaned back in a dramatic parody of abandonment. "Who cares?" she said. Bottingtonlike behavior, indeed. Was her husband still so concerned with "corporate image"? Even at a moment like this?

Suddenly, Mitch swept her into his arms. He moved determinedly down the hall and up the curving staircase. "What would our friends think if they saw me toting you around half-naked like this?" he whispered.

"They would envy us," she said fervently, reaching out to flick off the bedroom light as he kicked the door shut behind them.

Between that moment and dawn the next day, Clea occasionally giggled, occasionally pleaded with Mitch to stop, occasionally heard moans that she knew were her own but which seemed to come from far away. And while her husband did not escape unscathed, he did manage to keep the edge of control. It was a minor edge, but nevertheless there, Clea realized, waking quite late in the morning to find her workaholic spouse long since gone.

With the aid of the nanny who had been with him since his infancy, Kevin had apparently made his way off to school as well. After donning her yellow linen slacks and color-coordinated sweater tastefully stamped with a designer logo, Clea decided to occupy a few otherwise empty hours by catching up on some long-overdue letter writing.

But after a few desultory attempts to communicate society gossip and tidbits about Kevin's after-school activities, Clea resignedly placed her pen back in its holder. She didn't want to write letters. She wanted to work on her book.

Slipping on a pair of sandals, she smoothed back her hair, rolling it away from her face and catching it in an amber barrette. Her hair stylist must think she was on another European vacation, she mused. For appearance's sake, she'd better show up there soon. Before word got around and Mitch started wondering what she was doing with her free time.

Picking up her purse, keeping car keys in hand, Clea made her way quickly through the silent house. She stopped only briefly to tell the cook to make a light dinner, and to inform the maid that she'd be home before Kevin returned.

Even as she heard the dead-bolt lock on the double mahogany doors click behind her, Clea's mind was already elsewhere. Tanya was clad in a navy-blue business suit, complete with stark white blouse and tiny navy bow at the neck. Carrot hair like a beacon, patrician face flushed with anger, she confronted Tony in the sterile corridors that led to the main office of the large architectural design firm where she worked.

* * *

"When you asked permission to consult personally with my boss," she fumed, *"I expected you'd at least dress appropriately."*

"What's the matter with what I'm wearing?" Tony asked sardonically. *"Did I forget to tuck a doily in my pocket?"*

"I thought you and I had reached an understanding," Tanya snapped, the remnants of her morning calm dissolving around her.

"You mean because we happened to sleep together I'm supposed to knuckle under and put on a white shirt, tailored slacks, and prison tie?"

"Is that all it was to you?" Tanya asked, her face turning pale with fury under the smattering of freckles.

"If you'd stop confusing sex with love, we'd get along a lot more smoothly," Tony snarled, and the words hit Tanya like the flaying of a wet towel.

They also hit Clea that way. She slammed on the car brakes just as she was about to sail through a red light. Why, that was almost what she'd said to Mitch last night. With a slightly different slant, of course. But why had she said such a thing, anyway? It was in response to something he had asked, something about romance versus pornography . . .

Clea had to force herself to concentrate on stop signs and pedestrian traffic, as other memories from the delicious scene of the night before wafted through her consciousness. In the throes of passion, had Mitch really stopped to question what they were doing, complaining about the stuffed-shirt Bottington image once again? Indeed he had. Clea stiffened, tightening her grip on the wheel. What a bore! "Most un-Bottingtonlike behavior," was what he'd called it. Surely he wasn't questioning their newfound marital bliss. Surely he couldn't have been comparing their lovemaking sessions to pornography!

But as she climbed the few entry steps to the lavender-colored building, the blood pounding in her head, Clea had to admit that this was exactly what her infuriating spouse had done. Why, he'd even asked what their society acquaintances would think if . . . Clea flushed. The very idea! The Bottington image must not be allowed to intrude into the privacy of their very bedroom.

Clea closed the apartment door behind her, fussed with the coffeepot, and sipped the resulting steamy brew while looking out the window at a starling perched on a far branch of a poplar tree. Mitch had also said something about the Bottingtons' tendency toward philosophizing. Clearly, he'd been trying to make some Victorian point or other—but what? That abandonment in bed was not acceptable Bottington behavior? Well, he'd certainly enjoyed himself despite that . . . hadn't he?

Clea tried to shrug off her mounting anger, but as she sat down at the typewriter, Mitch's tone of the night before once again intruded into her consciousness. Only now it wasn't her husband speaking, it was his father. Eduard Livvright Bottington, who had laid down all those infuriating, iron-clad rules about the importance of image to Klectronics International.

Had Mitch been warning her? Letting her know that she was important, but the business was more so? Suddenly Clea was able to place that puzzling expression of Mitch's, to place it very well. It was the same expression he'd worn while delivering a lecture to her on the proper behavior of a Bottington wife, shortly before their marriage. At the time she'd thought it peculiar, but hadn't paid much attention. Now, however, she couldn't help wondering what place such proclamations had in their bedroom.

More furious even than Tanya, Clea threw the typewriter cover back on, pulled out the plug on the coffeepot with an abruptness that produced a shower of sparks, then slammed the apartment door behind her. She was halfway down the hall, and so absorbed in what she was going to tell Mitch, and how, that she didn't even notice Professor Tanners, who was coming along from the opposite direction carrying a full load of magazines.

The resulting collision floored Clea and her fellow tenant and sent the magazines flying in a dozen different directions. Clea hurried to rise, ignoring the sore spots that were sure to become bruises.

"I'm so sorry," she apologized.

"I thought that in my profession falling head over heels was out of the question," the professor joked, introducing himself for the first time and extending his hand with formal politeness.

Clea hurried to pick up the magazines, almost bumping into him again as she did so. "Calm down, young lady," he instructed tutorially. "It isn't good to race your way through anything in life, even a hallway."

"I was off to have an argument with my husband," Clea admitted shamefacedly. It didn't sound like a very good excuse for mowing someone down.

"Now why would you want to do that?" Professor Tanners asked, looking so pompously perturbed that Clea wanted to laugh.

"Because he puts business first and me a far-behind second," Clea blurted indignantly.

"Well, I don't know what shape his business is in," Professor Tanner said, "but you might suggest a visit to an optometrist so he can make an up-to-date comparison."

But Clea wasn't mollified. "I could win the Miss World beauty contest and my corporate-minded spouse would still put profits first."

"Are you quite certain of that?"

"Quite certain of what?"

"That money comes first." In his rumpled tweeds, Professor Tanners looked truly professorial, and although Clea really wanted to get on her way, she knew she had knocked the man's dignity enough for one day. She couldn't just leave.

Pausing for a moment, she shook her head. "What I said isn't quite true," Clea admitted. "Money is really not that important to Mitch. We have more than enough; and even if the firm were to close tomorrow, we would still have more than enough."

Professor Tanners seemed neither impressed nor surprised. "So what does he value?" he asked, the question phrased in such scholarly tones that Clea hesitated to marshal her thoughts before replying.

"The Klectronics corporate image," she said finally. "That's the name of his company."

"And what do you value?" Professor Tanners continued, his obvious concern forcing her to search for an honest answer.

"I really don't know," Clea admitted, her anger gone and in its place a curious heavyheartedness. "I always thought I valued whatever my husband did, but somehow, for some reason, that's no longer the case."

"Is that bad?"

"It doesn't seem fair to him. Mitch didn't marry a lunatic rebellious female who wanted nothing else but to lock herself away in a corner and write a steamy novel. He married a debutante from one of the city's finest families, who attended one of the most exclusive finishing schools, who showed every sign of being perfectly suited to the role of corporate wife. And look what he's got now!"

Professor Tanners's dark bushy eyebrows had risen slightly when Clea mentioned the word *novel*, but he let her finish her diatribe without interruption. Then, when he seemed reasonably sure she had nothing to add to her self-castigating monologue, he asked, "And what did *you* get?"

The question almost placed Clea back on her rear end again. Hands on her slim yellow-clad hips, she abruptly started to examine the problem from this other point of view. What *had* she gotten?

"I got a very handsome, very distinguished man who spends more time with his starched secretary than he does with me. I got a man who comes home so tired at night that he's asleep before he hits the bed. I got money when I already had enough money. I got designer dresses when I already had a closetful. I got—"

"Wait," Professor Tanners interrupted, finger poised in the air as though he were hushing a class. "Before you go any further with what you actually got, why don't you tell me what you thought you were getting?"

Clea's slowly emerging headache receded, and she took a deep, deliberate breath. "I married a man who could throw back his head in laughter. A man with a ready grin. A man who could give me an affectionate slap on the backside, one who was willing, even eager, to talk to me as if I were a human being and not a Klectronics subsidiary. I married a man who loved me and wasn't afraid to show it, out of the house or inside. I married Mitchell Eduard Bottington, human being— not Mitchell Eduard Bottington, public-relations machine."

She paused for a few seconds, then drew herself up into almost military posture and asked, "Does that answer your question?"

"No," Professor Tanners replied. "It answers yours."

"I don't understand," Clea protested. But she did understand. All too well. Mitchell had changed; and if he had a right to change, so did she. It wasn't only a question of what was fair to him but of what was fair to her.

"I should collide with you more often," Clea said, her mood lightening as if by magic.

"Not today, please," Professor Tanners said rather hastily. "Besides, didn't I hear you say something about getting back to work on your novel? You *are* writing a novel?"

"Oh, yes," Clea exclaimed with a quick glance at her watch. "I had the most terrific scene going during my drive here. If I don't hurry, I won't get it down on paper in time."

"Good day," Professor Tanners said with a slight nod.

Clea, halfway down the hall already, turned toward him and waved. Her face was as shining and happy as the sun-colored outfit she wore. She couldn't wait to get Tony and Tanya alone in that executive boardroom.

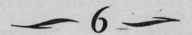

6

FINGERS FLYING ACROSS the keyboard as if swept by magic, Clea found her story moving almost of its own accord. Tanya was learning there was more to life than a devotion to architecture, no matter how hard-won her entrée into the profession had been. And Tony was learning that there was at least one female in the world who could be attracted by his overt masculinity yet refuse to prostrate herself like a doormat at his feet.

By page 123, the two characters were in the process of learning even more about themselves and each other. The scene was set in the plushly carpeted corporate boardroom. Tanya was minus her tidy dark blue neck bow. Her stark white blouse was unbuttoned to the waist. The clock on the wall said 6:10. Everyone but she and Tony had left the building over an hour ago. From the beads of moisture on Tanya's forehead to the way Tanya was clutching the table behind her, Clea was able to paint a verbal portrait of her heroine that made it clear to the reader she wasn't going anyplace at all. Except to bed with her hero. Eventually, of course.

"Don't you ever stop thinking of yourself as a stud service?" Tanya hissed, making no attempt to disguise the rapid rise and fall of her small firm breasts, now partially exposed.

"Why don't you stop objecting to what's good for you?" Tony countered, pulling his T-shirt over his massive shoulders and flinging it across the silent room.

"Fold it," Tanya instructed.

"I beg your pardon?" Tony questioned, so astonished by the unexpected instruction that the lecherous leer disappeared from his face.

"I told you to fold your shirt," Tanya repeated authoritatively. "This isn't some five-second roll in the hay. We have an hour or more until the janitor arrives. So you can at least be a gentleman about it."

Tony considered himself as worldly-wise as any man, and possibly more so considering his varied and frequent bedroom experiences. But this woman, this female, this girl-child who frequently dressed like a man—and spoke like one—was beginning to get to him.

She wasn't refusing to sleep with him. She'd already done that, a while ago. Nor did she bother to deny his irresistible attraction.

No, it was something even more ridiculous, and hitherto unknown. Tanya was more than willing to have sex with him—provided he behaved like a good little boy. If his buddies at the shop ever heard about this, they'd laugh themselves silly.

Tony started to walk across the room, fully intending to put his shirt back on and walk right out the door. However, as he bent to retrieve the crumpled mass of cotton, he glanced back over his broad shoulder at what he was about to walk away from. Carrot top or not, she *looked pretty good. Tony picked up his shirt and folded it into a neat square, then placed it decorously on the seat of a nearby chair.*

"Do your jeans the same way," Tanya instructed. It wasn't quite a command, but Tony got the definite impression that rapid compliance was expected.

"What is this, a strip show?" he inquired irritably.

"Why don't you stop objecting to what's good for you?" Tanya asked, mimicking his own earlier remark.

There was the merest of smiles on her face. After Tony considered her words for a few seconds, he allowed a slight smile to soften his own countenance. A few seconds later it was followed by a baritone roar of laughter.

"Hush," cautioned Tanya, putting a slim finger to her lips.

"Why?" Tony asked with mock seriousness. "We have at least an hour until the janitor arrives. Make that forty-five minutes."

Tanya glanced at the wall clock. "Right you are," she said in precise tones, slipping out of her tailored dark blue skirt and folding it neatly.

Tony's muscular arms were wrapped around her waist before she could proceed either forward or back. Lifting her up, he seated her on the polished oval walnut table.

"Hard surfaces are good for the back," he said casually as he deftly removed her nylons.

Now it was Tanya's turn to express astonishment. "The table?" she asked incredulously, trying to figure out how Tony had managed to unhook her brassiere so deftly.

"The floor's too dusty," Tony said, his lecherous leer returning.

Tanya, watching Tony fold her stark white bra and panties carefully on a chair, didn't know what to think. But seconds after he'd flipped off the light, her worries abruptly vanished.

* * *

Clea's rapid-fire typing ceased just as abruptly. A quick glance at her Tiffany watch told her that Kevin would be home in a very short while. Although the maids and his nanny were there, Clea always made it a point to be home to greet her son after school. A small gesture perhaps, considering that he usually left almost immediately to visit a neighborhood friend or arrived with David and Boppo only to disappear into his room with his computer games, but a gesture she chose to make, nonetheless.

Replacing the cover on her typewriter, Clea followed her usual routine of cleaning the coffeepot, collecting the usual heap of crumpled papers in a garbage bag to be thrown away, and checking the windows to make sure they were locked.

On impulse, she reread the last page she'd typed. Not bad, she decided. Or was it? she wondered suddenly. What if one of her readers had actually made love on an oval walnut table? Would such a reader find her description somehow inaccurate?

Oh, dear. That meant she would have to enlist Mitch's aid again. But how on earth would she ever get him onto a table? It would have to be the dining-room table, she mused, since the one in the kitchen was rectangular and rather small.

Of course, Clea mused, if she could make herself look as good as her heroine Tanya, then maybe Mitch wouldn't protest too vehemently. Clea tried to imagine her husband not protesting at all, but her imagination didn't take her that far. Her hero Tony was a construction worker accustomed to a bit of rough and tumble, while Mitch was a corporate executive accustomed to ironed sheets. She couldn't expect the same behavior from Mitch. In fact, her success in getting him onto the carpeted floor despite the "Bottington image" was a minor miracle in itself.

But a table? That would require even more ingenuity on her part.

Her amusement got the better of her, and Clea was chuckling to herself as she climbed into her Rolls Royce. But her mirth ceased abruptly when she noticed the parking ticket stuck under the windshield wiper.

Impossible, Clea thought angrily. But a quick glance around revealed that she was indeed parked in a loading zone. Her thoughts had been so focused on Tony and Tanya that she hadn't even noticed the sign. Clea sighed. The San Francisco police were obviously out in full force that afternoon.

With a slight shrug of her slim shoulders—after all, a parking ticket was hardly a calamity—Clea tucked the slip of paper into her leather purse. She'd send a check off tomorrow. No need to fuss. She had more important things to think about.

The traffic was light, and her thoughts continued to sort themselves out like patterns in a kaleidoscope. She wanted to complete the table scene as soon as possible— hopefully, the following morning, bright and early. That meant she'd have to set the scene with Mitch this very evening. But after Mitch's prudish remarks about romance and pornography last night, she feared it might well be a case of too much, too soon.

Clea mulled that over while staring at two interminable cycles of a red light. Should she give her husband a rest, or pursue her advantage before she lost it altogether? A famous army officer had once said, "When in doubt, attack." While she preferred not to think of her amorous escapades in such a militant light, the motto seemed apt nonetheless. Mitch was already beginning to balk. If she gave him more time to contemplate the Bottington image, who knew what might happen?

That matter taken care of, Clea tucked it away in her mental filing cabinet. But finding herself stuck behind a double-parked car that blocked her lane, she withdrew another problem from that same file, and proceeded to chew it over. The novel, she thought, was well on its way to completion. No longer simply the product of a "dare," the project had become a legitimate enterprise. Wasn't it time to further legitimize it by making a bid for publication? Or didn't Clea Witherspoon Bottington, socialite wife of prominent and conservative Mitchell Eduard Bottington, have the guts to try and market her titillating tale?

At the mere thought, every ancestor from her impeccable genealogy suddenly seemed to bombard her with ghostly messages of horror. She could imagine what a field day the newspaper columnists would have when the news leaked out. Lurid headlines—WIFE OF ELECTRONICS WIZARD WRITES OF PEAKED NIPPLES—would scream from the local papers. There'd go the all-important Bottington image, right down the drain. And she could just picture Mitch's face when he noted the similarities between Tony and Tanya's courtship and the seemingly spontaneous interludes he had shared with Clea. Romance and pornography, indeed!

As she pulled the Rolls into the driveway, the pros and cons of the issue were zinging back and forth across her mind like Ping-Pong balls at a tournament. No, she wouldn't; it was just a lark anyhow. Yes, she would; after all, she had put a lot of labor into the book. No, she wouldn't; her family would be so embarrassed. Yes, she would; she was entitled to a life of her own. No, she wouldn't; she couldn't write anyhow. Yes, she would; she had faith in herself.

In the end, it was a telephone message that resolved the issue. "Mrs. DomPeter would like you to return her call," the maid informed Clea as she entered the house.

What does that busybody want? Clea wondered, inwardly debating the wisdom of pretending she hadn't received the message. A useless ploy, she eventually decided. Mrs. DomPeter would just keep badgering her until she got what she wanted. Whatever it was. With a resigned sigh, Clea checked the number and dialed.

"Darling," Mrs. DomPeter gushed, "how sweet of you to call back right away. If I ever get a chance to chat with your busy husband, I'll let him know how lucky he is to have you."

Mrs. DomPeter sounded in fine form. She had probably fired her entire staff of servants again, this time on the grounds that they breathed too much air or tiptoed too loudly. Having thus cleansed her eighteen-room estate of all life but that of her five cats, she would have nobody nearby to plague and would have to look outside for her victims—hence, no doubt, her call. Clea sighed.

Mrs. DomPeter soon zeroed in on her topic. "I hear that upstanding young husband of yours is finally going to do something about that travesty of sexual education in the schools."

At first Clea hadn't a clue as to what Mrs. DomPeter was talking about. But as the quarrelsome dowager launched into a discourse on the evils of "scurrilous literature," Clea began to get an inkling. Mrs. DomPeter's definition of that term seemed to include anything remotely pertaining to the human body below the neck, and as she ranted on, Clea felt prickles of annoyance creeping up her spine.

"I really can't see what's so awful about a normal human function," Clea managed to squeeze in during pauses in Mrs. DomPeter's diatribe.

"You don't mean sex, my dear, do you?" came the shocked response. Mrs. DomPeter enunciated the word *sex* as if she was referring to something lifted from the bottom of a humus pile.

"Actually, I do," Clea said, fighting down a strong impulse to hang up the receiver.

There was a funereal silence at the other end of the line. "I see," said Mrs. DomPeter at last.

"Well, you were married," Clea volleyed, knowing full well she should shut up.

"Oh, that business." The dowager sniffed. "Certainly it's permissible within the confines of fulfilling one's obligatory marital duties. I thought you were talking about single people."

A tiny warning voice told Clea to keep quiet, but to no avail. "Them, too," she said a bit too casually. Her mind flitted to an image of the late Mr. DomPeter. No wonder he'd always seemed so unhappy.

"Disgusting," Mrs. DomPeter said vehemently.

"What's disgusting?" Clea asked.

"Voluntary commission of the sex act," Mrs. DomPeter responded tartly.

"How on earth would you commit it involuntarily?" Clea couldn't help inquiring. The inner voices telling her to shut up were getting louder and clearer. Too late, Clea bit her lip. Had she really said that?

"I beg your pardon?" Mrs. DomPeter queried.

"Never mind," responded Clea, hoping against hope that Mrs. DomPeter hadn't heard correctly.

There was an extended silence on the other end of the line. Finally, Mrs. DomPeter coughed once, then twice. "Do I understand you to imply you're in opposition to your husband's policies?" the woman asked icily.

"Are you referring to the Parent-Teacher Liaison Group brouhaha over censorship?" Clea said. "Well . . . I'd say Mitch's views on that, um, need to be clarified."

"Oh," said Mr. DomPeter. There were a few coughs, the sharp click of a cigarette lighter, and then a few more coughs.

"I never did ask why you called," Clea remarked, regarding her fingernails. She could think of lots of things she'd rather be doing than talking to Mrs. DomPeter on the phone. And the longer this conversation went on, the more likely she was to say something inappropriate.

"Actually, I was going to ask you to appear with your husband on a P.T.L.G. panel presenting the anti-slime viewpoint," Mrs. DomPeter replied, her gravelly voice holding more than a hint of malice.

Clea had the definite feeling she was being set up, but she didn't know for quite what.

"But since you obviously can't help us with that, my dear," the dowager concluded, "perhaps you'd be willing to pour the lemonade."

The sound of a receiver being replaced clicked abruptly in Clea's ear. She groaned. The gentle inner voices she'd been ignoring were now those of vaudeville singers, working with megaphones. Why on earth hadn't she just kept quiet? Then she sighed. Anti-slime viewpoint, indeed. She supposed that Mrs. DomPeter would consider the foibles of Tanya and Tony slime. Well, Mrs. DomPeter was wrong. Tanya and Tony were just two people from two different backgrounds who happened to love each other very much, even if they had a terrible time admitting it. If their story was slimy, then she, Clea, would have to take the pro-slime position.

Suddenly, she snapped to attention, squaring her shoulders with a new burst of conviction. No, she thought, there wasn't a thing wrong with what she'd written. It was an entertainment, something to brighten the dull evenings of women who had no one to come home to at night, or women whose husbands worked as frantically as hers did. Blinking away the vision of Bottington and Witherspoon ancestors perched side by side on the fence post of her mind, Clea made her final decision. She would send the partial manuscript off tomorrow.

Just then Kevin bounded in, wanting dinner. Was it that late already? It was. He had been to a scout meeting. Had she forgotten? She had.

"Go ask Cook," Clea said, hugging the towheaded little boy.

Kevin brushed himself off with first-grade masculine dignity. "I hope it's hot dogs," he said.

"Seems to me it's escargot," she said cheerfully. All of a sudden she felt light-headed, as though a tremendous burden had been lifted from her shoulders. She could hardly wait for tomorrow.

As Kevin disappeared into the kitchen, the telephone sounded once, twice. Clea listened to the shrill ring, decided it was probably Mrs. DomPeter calling back, and let the maid answer it. She wasn't in the mood for any more of the dowager's criticism.

When she was halfway up the stairs, the maid called her. Standing prim and starched on the balcony overhead, the girl wore a hand-knit cardigan and was obviously ready to leave for the day. "Your husband's on the phone," she announced.

"I'll take it in my room," Clea responded, her heart skipping in anticipation like that of a schoolgirl's.

Mitch's first sentence was totally unexpected. In her lovely sun-yellow sweater and sun-yellow slacks, her sun-colored hair caught in a golden barrette, Clea felt her face turn the hue of ice in midwinter.

"Mrs. DomPeter just phoned me," Mitch began with no other greeting.

The tolling of the death knell could not possibly be heard in the palatial Bottington mansion in Hampstead Estates, set apart from the rest of the city by thick walls and gates, yet somehow Clea heard it. "She called here a while ago," she murmured softly, not knowing what else to say.

"Mrs. DomPeter, as you are well aware, has been a most generous donor to the school's various fund-raising activities," Mitch went on coldly.

Clea was well aware. She waited.

Mitch continued in a monotone, as if he were so furious it was the only way to keep his anger in check.

"Mrs. DomPeter, who is also on the boards of several other worthy San Francisco charities, has planned to set up a formal debate between the two opposing factions on this book issue." There was another pause. Clea still did not respond. How could a lump of clay with its heart in its mouth respond? She could almost hear what was coming before her husband said it.

"Mrs. DomPeter is going ahead with the debate," Mitch persevered punishingly. "Only you won't be sitting on my side of the table."

"Mitch—" Clea tried to interrupt, but Mitch wouldn't allow it.

"Instead," he continued acerbically, "the wife of Klectronics International's president, Mitchell Bottington, will be speaking for the opposition. Mrs. DomPeter feels that this will be good publicity. Good for her fund-raising efforts. That it will draw a terrific crowd. I'm afraid I couldn't disagree . . ."

Clea didn't know why she had ever thought of hell as a remote place, peopled by grinning demons with red-hot pitchforks. Hell was her own bedroom with its fluffy down comforter, its plush rug, its double mirrors, both reflecting her ashen face.

"You . . . you mean you agreed to that?" she whispered.

"What choice did I have?" Mitch railed.

"Mitch, I didn't say anything untoward, you must believe me. It's just that her views are simply archaic. Why, according to Mrs. DomPeter, even within the confines of marriage, a wife shouldn't—"

"That's enough," Mitch said, his voice hot with apparent embarrassment. Clea could imagine Miss Hoven waiting, all ears, in the office nearby.

"Suffice it to say," he resumed, practically whispering, "that my taking on the presidency of the Parent-Teachers Liaison Group was strictly for business reasons, to enhance the image of Klectronics. I believe I made that quite clear from the beginning. And now you're defeating my very purpose. You're making a mockery of me, Clea. You're making a mockery of Klectronics International. And I won't stand for it."

"Yes," said Clea bitingly. "I believe you and Sonora Cameron did a duet on that subject several days ago. "And, if you recall, I wasn't very enthusiastic about your taking on that project."

"What has Sonora got to do with all this?" Mitch snapped. Clea wondered why her reference to the purchasing manager should bother him. Miss Cameron should, according to the best of her calculations, be long since gone.

"Well," she offered petulantly, "Sonora wouldn't have done anything so unprofessional as to contradict the head of every important charity in San Francisco, now would she? The prig. Maybe you should have married *her*."

"Sonora," shouted Mitch, "respects the Klectronics image, first and foremost. As do I. As did my father before me. Just as I expect *you*, my wife, to do. It's part of your job, part of our marital contract. And I have every right to assume you will uphold it. And without any more ridiculous cracks about one of my most dedicated employees!"

Clea doubted that many people had ever hung up on the illustrious Mitchell Bottington. It was even possible that she was the first to do so. But as she slammed the receiver into its cradle with a satisfying bang, she told herself that she didn't regret it. Not in the least.

But just as quickly as it had arisen, her anger cooled. Perhaps Mitch's expectations were not so unrealistic, considering the attitudes they'd both held at the time of their marriage. The problem was that she seemed to have changed. Who was she now, anyway?

Clea had no ready answer to that question, but she did know one thing: she wouldn't be just another Klectronics clone. She'd be a person in her own right, she thought rebelliously, a person who earned her *own* accolades.

Images of Tanya and Tony began to fade in and out, as though a movie projector were focused on her brain. "My book is good," she announced to no one in particular. "In fact, it's great," she decided. "It's a terrific book!"

Again she turned to stare at the silent phone. Mitch would be furious. Furious that she'd hung up on him, furious that she'd somehow involved him in Mrs. DomPeter's stupid debate scheme. Well, he could have refused if he felt that way. His overweening concern with his corporate image was his own problem.

Clea sank down onto the plush-covered bed. She'd have to soothe his ruffled feathers, she thought with a sigh. But just then an idea caused a devilish smile to break out on her face. She realized she had the perfect solution to all her problems—including Mitch.

There were decided advantages to having plenty of money, Clea acknowledged to herself an hour later. Among them was the ability to pick up the phone and order whatever oddment you wanted and have it delivered after hours, right then and there. Had the furniture store owner thought her request strange? she wondered. Perhaps so, but that hadn't kept him from filling her order for an oval, mahogany table, without the legs, please.

Said table now lay ostentatiously on the floor of the living room. Kevin had watched the delivery proceedings with great interest but, in the manner of children, had taken this adult idiosyncrasy in his stride.

"Are you and Daddy going to use it to play backgammon on?" he asked, a clearly plausible idea from his play-oriented point of view.

"Daddy and I are going to use it for games," Clea said, wondering if her evasion would provoke further comment. It didn't. Kevin lost interest immediately.

"Can I go watch TV now?" he inquired.

"One more program before bedtime," Clea acquiesced. She had no way of knowing when Mitch would arrive, but it wouldn't hurt to let Kevin exhaust himself with an extra hour of TV. The more soundly asleep he was when Clea led her husband to the living room, the better.

Two hours later, Kevin was fast asleep and Clea had had a good long soak in the tub. There would be no pretense about what she wanted tonight, she thought, donning a persimmon terry-cloth robe over nothing at all.

She brushed her still-damp hair off her face, debated whether to wear lipstick, decided against it, but added cream blusher in a pattern that emphasized her almost Oriental cheekbones. By the time her toilette was complete, she had decided on using the direct approach with Mitch.

They could, she would explain as if it were all completely ordinary, make love on the regular dining-room table, or they could try the lower version first. It reduced the whole issue to a simple problem of logistics, she thought craftily. Surely Mitch would see it that way.

But first she'd better pave the way for such an amiable confrontation. She dialed his private line and was gratified when Mitch picked up.

"I'm sorry about the debate, darling," she purred. "Perhaps Mrs. DomPeter will reconsider and—"

"I don't want to talk about it," Mitch snapped. "At all. When the time comes for the debate, I'll have figured out the proper course of action. In the meantime, I don't want to hear one more word on the subject."

"Yes, dear," Clea said agreeably.

"And Clea," he said, a trace of wounded pride apparent in his voice, "I never want you to hang up on me again."

"No, darling," said Clea, genuinely contrite. "I hope you'll be home soon; I'll make it up to you."

"By letting me get some sleep, I hope," Mitch said, a trifle huffily, Clea thought. Never mind. She'd take care of that.

An hour later Clea found her direct approach wasn't working especially well. "I'm not suggesting we make love while skiing," she said patiently. "I'm not suggesting we sit on top of an elephant."

"That's only because you haven't found an elephant, and you don't know how to ski," Mitch replied exasperatedly. "I can't believe this entire series of weird activities is really coming from you. At first I thought it was a temporary effort to alleviate boredom. But now I'm beginning to suspect you spend your entire day thinking up these off-the-wall contortions."

"Contortions?" Clea echoed with raised brows. "Oh, come now, Mitch. You spend a fortune trying to improve electronics equipment—inventing, experimenting, testing. Yet when I try the same procedure at home, you act as if I'm going mad."

"It's not the same," Mitch denied.

"Why not?" Clea asked, lying down on the table. Still clad in her brilliant robe, she raised one shapely leg in the air for his inspection.

"Because," Mitch replied. However, Clea sensed that her logic was beginning to make some sense to him. Considering it was all ad-lib, she was rather pleased with herself. She was merely improving a product. And if the product happened to be sex . . . well, that was certainly more interesting than electronics equipment.

But Clea didn't say this. Instead she inquired, "Because why?"

The very uncorporate pink blush began wending its way up above Mitch's white shirt collar. Pretending it was due to the overheated house, he loosened his tie. Clea liked the way he loosened his tie. More men should wear ties so they could take them off, she mused. Her hero Tony would wear a tie tomorrow. She decided all this while putting one leg down and slowly lifting the other in the air.

"You do have great ankles," Mitch commented appreciatively, at the same time attempting to look stern. Poor husband, Clea thought sympathetically. It's going to be very difficult for him to chastise me about Mrs. DomPeter while his subconscious is trying to get a good peek up my bathrobe.

However, true to form, Mitch made a valiant effort. "I want you to stop offering your opinion on the schoolbooks issue," he stated. "Also, while we're on the subject, you should apologize to Mrs. DomPeter."

Clea sat up on the polished mahogany table and pushed the top portion of her robe over her shoulders, letting it drape around her waist. She crossed her legs and sat Indian-style, hand resting lightly on her knees.

"That's not fair," Mitch objected. The objection was accompanied by a discreet change in the contour of his tailored blue slacks.

"Would you like me to tell Mrs. DomPeter I agree with her?"

"Agree about what?" Mitch said suspiciously.

Like putty in my hands, Clea thought triumphantly, taking care to remain serene and unmoving. "That voluntary commission of the sexual act, in or out of marriage, is disgusting," she replied.

"Aren't you exaggerating somewhat?" Mitch asked, trying his best to focus on the conversation.

"Do you remember poor Chauncey DomPeter?" Clea asked, changing position so that she lay flat on the table.

Mitch didn't seem to want to remember poor Mr. DomPeter. His own mate had her bare arms folded under her head, the position accentuating the line of her rib cage and the delectable ruby-tipped roundness of her breasts.

He removed his shirt, started to throw it on a nearby chair, then hesitated and asked, "Do I have to fold it?"

Clea laughed so hard she had to roll over to catch her breath. In that semiprone position her ivory body looked as if it had stepped out of a classical oil painting. Mitch knelt down and ran his fingers over her spinal column, from her neck to the cleft between her firm buttocks.

Clea tilted her face to grin mischievously at him. "No," she replied. "Folding was last night. Each night we have to try something different."

Mitch was nibbling at her ear, while his deft, powerful hands did some random exploration of bodily areas above and below her robe.

"That tickles." Clea giggled as the warm wetness of his tongue traced a duplicate pattern from the curve of her neck to the indentation of her waist.

"My knees hurt," Mitch retorted, reclining on the table and rolling her on top of him.

"Well, your belt buckle is boring a hole through my stomach," Clea protested, staring down at the mahogany table, while she rubbed her bare foot against her husband's calf.

"Can't we compromise?" Mitch inquired huskily, taking pretend, man-size bites out of her shoulder.

"What type of compromise?"

As Clea had expected, Mitch pleaded with her to adjourn to the bedroom, something she absolutely would not consider.

Mitch stubbornly retaliated by shifting their positions

so that Clea was now lying beneath him on her stomach. Mitch wasn't exactly a featherweight at 180 pounds, and Clea began to wonder if her table scenario was really feasible. But she wasn't about to give up yet.

"Tell you what," she counter-offered, realizing that if Mitch put his full weight on her, instead of propping himself up on his elbows, she would be summarily squashed.

"What?" Mitch asked absently, brushing her hair off the nape of her neck and tracing the hairline with his lips.

Quaking with a pleasure that overrode her discomfort, Clea negotiated: "If you'll take every stitch of your clothing off, and lie there on the table for two minutes, on your back, I'll agree to transfer to a more plush location."

"No sooner said than done, " Mitch said, rising to strip off his slacks and form-fitting underwear.

Clea stood on the sidelines and watched as Mitch assumed a position of total repose on the expensive tabletop. His arms were cradled under his head and the dark tufts of curly hair peeked out from under his well-muscled shoulders.

The word *sensuous* couldn't adequately describe this Adonis, framed by a mahogany sheen. He presented a total, unadulteratedly virile invitation. In an unexpected turnabout, it was Clea who suddenly found herself blushing.

How odd, she thought, knowing Mitch was watching her with unabashed amusement. She had been married to this man for eight years. In the course of their daily life she had seen him in the bedroom, in the bathroom, during times of health and bouts of illness. His body was almost as familiar to her as her own. So why did it look so different now?

"Do I pass inspection?" Mitch teased, interrupting her thoughts.

"I wasn't inspecting you," Clea denied, pretending to be offended as she noted that he had awfully nice legs for a man. They were long, well muscled but not overly so, and had just the right amount of soft, downy hair on the thighs and calves.

"Then you must be counting the hairs on my knees," Mitch observed with wry amusement.

"You don't have any hair on your knees," Clea objected, moving closer for a double check.

"Are you absolutely positive?" Mitch asked, feigning perplexity.

"Positive!" Clea emphasized, verifying her statement by sitting down on the table beside him to peer nearsightedly at his legs.

"It must have evaporated," he said in astonished tones, a cherubic look on his face. That expression seemed singularly out of sync with the long-lashed smoky eyes and the slightly demonic tilt to the corner of his mouth. The tilt turned into a full grin as he added, "Why don't you check the hairs on my chest and see if they're still in place?"

"I'll count them," Clea announced, nuzzling Mitch's broad chest with her mouth. "Mmm," she murmured moments later, her cheek against his warm abdomen.

"Hey, don't get carried away. My two minutes were up about ten minutes ago."

"Um," Clea murmured again, producing a marked reaction by using just the tip of her tongue to circle the hollow of his navel.

It occurred to her in passing that the lushness of their bedroom would be many times more comfortable than the polished hardness of this table on the floor. Then again, the setting had so far proved to be a tremendous turn-on.

Clea's darting tongue explored Mitch's navel and its environs. A fiery wave traveled up from her toes, inch by inch, destroying everything in its path until her lower limbs seemed not to exist at all.

As she consumed Mitch with her mouth, savoring the damp salty flesh of him—his arms, his back, the tiny roseate prickles of his nipples—the heat of desire seemed to build in her until she felt she would explode. Still she avoided the pulsating center of his being, moving around it, tantalizing it, never satisfying his increasingly urgent demand.

Mitch's broad chest was damp with perspiration now as his large hands kneaded Clea's supple skin. He has amazing self-control, she thought fleetingly, as she found yet another way to test that discipline.

"Enough," Mitch cried after a few seconds of her erotic torment. He pulled Clea roughly on top of him, placing the palms of his hands on each side of her face to bring it down to his.

Then it was Mitch's turn to torment and demand, to titillate and tease. His mouth became the center of a tornado, drawing everything to it, allowing nothing to escape. Clea could barely breathe. Yet when Mitch finally released her, she wanted nothing more than to seek that darkness again.

His fingers were viselike on her moist, sensitized flesh; she dared not cry out for fear he would stop.

"Damn crazy woman," Mitch moaned, moving her onto his throbbing need. Clea's whimpers were gentle at first as he undulated within her, searching out her weaknesses, making her cry for more.

Then the soft moans became more urgent as her fingernails dug into his back, urging him ever deeper into her core. She was a volcano on the brink of eruption, an eruption that would destroy her very being with such splendor that she could only beg for it to happen.

Then, without warning, the molten flow turned the night into day, illuminating Clea's world like some cosmic camera flash, encompassing the whole universe in its visual framework. The burning lava shot into the atmosphere, cascaded to a peak, arched, and moved downward, searing every millimeter of flesh within its path.

Clea remained where she was until an increasingly sharp pain in her knees brought her to the realization that she was still on the table. "Ouch," she said, rolling onto the carpeted floor.

"Ouch," Mitch echoed, not moving. There was a supremely happy smile on his face, like that of a kid who had just hit a home run, right over the fence.

"What are you complaining about?" Clea asked playfully, scooting over to rest her body on the plush carpet while placing her head on his outstretched arm. "You had it easier than I did."

"Well, one of us had to get the comfortable position," he observed frankly, twisting slightly to give her an affectionate kiss on the cheek.

That little gesture of affection actually pleased Clea more than the rapture they had just shared. Mitch wasn't generally one for tenderness, and it was especially welcome now. Like real whipped cream on top of a super double-fudge chocolate cake.

"Gee, thanks," she said.

"Don't mention it," Mitch replied with a straight face. Then, innocently, he added, "You can leave my tip on the table."

"Beast!" She retaliated by tickling his stomach.

"I should hope so," he managed, roaring with laughter as he moved to tickle her back. At that moment, he rolled off the table.

During the jocular wrestling match that ensued, Clea made a mental note: Don't let Tony tickle Tanya on the table or there'll be one big crash!

Much later, she asked herself how she could possibly think of her novel in the midst of an amorous session with her spouse. But after she had brushed her teeth and was looking into the mirror, she realized she had half expected to see her feisty, carrot-topped heroine instead of the ash-blond and theoretically serene Clea Bottington.

It's as if I'm living two lives, Clea thought, slipping silently between the sheets. Mitch was sleeping peacefully and she tried not to disturb him. Yet as she settled into place he murmured drowsily, "How did you get that bruise on your backside? I didn't do that, did I?"

Clea was about to ask "What bruise?" when she remembered her painful collision with Professor Tanners in the apartment house hall.

"I tripped on the throw rug in the entryway," she replied, yawning. By the time she turned over, Mitch was already sound asleep.

7

"Mrs. Bottington, why did you tell your husband you tripped on that rug in the entryway?"

The tone was aggrieved, and Clea looked up from her newspaper to be confronted by the gardener's wife, who came in several times a week to do the heavier cleaning jobs.

"I don't know," she replied with a shrug. "He asked me where I had bruised my hip, and I was really tired and didn't feel like thinking, so I blamed the rug. It's really not important."

"It may not be important to you, Mrs. Bottington, but it is to me. Your husband told me several weeks ago to make certain that rug was fixed so no one would trip on it. And I did fix it. Now he thinks I lied to him."

Clea concentrated on the steaming mug of coffee she held in her hand. She counted to ten, then twenty. Why do people have to make mountains out of molehills? she thought irritably. But she merely responded, "You're perfectly correct. I remember now. I tripped in the driveway while bringing some packages into the house. Sorry if I caused you any problem."

Clea offered several profuse apologies, all of which were grudgingly accepted when she promised to tell Mitch the truth. Then she tossed the matter out of her consciousness as she gave her full attention to a lengthy article on the well-decorated boudoir.

"If your love life is losing its zip," the article read, "the fault could lie with your furniture." The reporter went on to quote an A.I.D. decorator, who suggested starting small with such accoutrements as ceiling mirrors, silk pillows, hanging plants, and moving on, when possible, to a round bed.

Before she began her novel, Clea would never have bothered with such an article. Even if she had, by chance, read one, she would have considered it just so much foolishness. And very tacky, of course.

Now, however, she read the piece three times over, her delight growing with each perusal. A bedroom fit for a sultan would surely be a fine addition to her book. Yet how could she fit it into the plot?

She was still mulling the matter over as she reminded Kevin that clean shirt and slacks were a step in the right direction, but that he also had to change his socks each day. She was no closer to a solution when the car-pool driver honked impatiently in the driveway and Kevin raced out the door. And although visions of mirrors, pillows, and potted palms danced before her eyes on her drive to her apartment, she could think of no likely reason for utilitarian Tanya or tough Tony to have such tawdry decor. Unless . . .

By the time she reached the lavender building, a gray rain had started to fall; but Clea was feeling positively ebullient. On the way there she had stopped and purchased two small ivy plants, a pair of candles, a cheap sateen pillow, and the least expensive mirror she could find. These she arranged by her typewriter.

After making her routine pot of coffee and opening the window to ventilate the place, Clea took out a clean sheet of paper and began typing.

She got Tony and Tanya out of the executive board-room in six steamy pages. Two pages later they were getting along so well that Tony suggested they spend the weekend at his vacation cabin in the mountains.

Tanya, thinking about all that fresh air and the prospect of some good fishing, enthusiastically agreed. She packed her oldest clothes, including sneakers with holes in the toes and a small container for worms. She even tucked in a harmonica saved from childhood, in case the nights got long.

Clea's heroine was looking forward to getting to know her hero better in a natural setting, away from the trappings of civilization. Therefore, when five pages later they arrived at Tony's cabin, she was totally flabbergasted by the sight that greeted her.

"What on earth?" Tanya exclaimed, gaping at the floor-to-ceiling gold-veined mirrors that lined both bedroom and bathroom.

"Like it?" Tony chuckled, picking up one of the immense red satin heart-shaped pillows and tossing it across the room.

It landed on the bed, which was immense, round, and covered in red velvet.

"I can't even comprehend it," Tanya replied, her eyes taking in the brass headboard with a row of red and white candles placed in holders along its upper rim.

Clea got up from her typewriter, lit the two candles she had brought along for atmosphere, and placed the mirror in an upright position so she could see her own reflection. Then she walked around the room alternately stroking the sateen pillow and picking up and putting down the two ivy plants she had brought. Deciding she now had it down pat, she returned to her manuscript.

"Well, to tell the truth," Tony retorted, *"when Cecilia first did it, I wasn't too thrilled. But . . . after you get used to it, it really adds something to the bedroom experience."*

"Who or what is Cecilia?" Tanya inquired icily.

Oh good, thought Clea, they're going to get into another fight. The kissing and making up was always so lovely. And it would be especially nice in a bedroom like this one!

Clack-clack-clack. The keys struck the white paper, stamping out their tiny hieroglyphics, and then moved on. Cecilia, it seems, was one of Tony's many former girl friends. Professionally, she was an interior decorator. Psychologically, she was a bit of a flake, who positively freaked out on the color red.

Four tempestuous pages later, Clea had concluded the splendid fight between Tanya and Tony. It featured a furious red-satin-pillow fight, three candles, and a potted plant being thrown across the room with such force that a mirrored tile shattered; and it concluded with a resounding slam of the front door through which Tanya made her heel-clattering exit.

What next? Clea sat back in her chair, deep in thought. Well, first, Tanya would insist on redecorating the bedroom immediately.

What style would she choose? Probably tartan plaids and crisp corners, Clea decided with a tinge of dismay. There was nothing she could really do to change her heroine's mind. Fictional characters did tend to develop personalities of their own. They didn't allow an author to push them around.

Oh well, it would be easy enough for her to write a scene about room redecoration. She had certainly gone through the process often enough.

Clea put the cover back on her typewriter. She'd accomplished enough for one day, more in fact than she'd ever done before in a single sitting.

She made herself a last cup of coffee. After opening the box of imported English biscuits, she dotted them lightly with Scottish marmalade. She figured she had a half hour in which to relax.

But as she sipped her coffee in its porcelain cup, her eyes roved back to the manuscript on her desk. *Secret Diary of Delights*. She read the title page absently. Was it just yesterday that she'd made the decision to try and sell it?

Now she stared at the sheaf of papers and wondered if it was really a good idea. She supposed she could go on forever trying to make up her mind. One day, yes; the next day, no.

Impulsively she removed a large, padded manilla envelope from the lower desk drawer. On it she placed several dollars' worth of stamps, then printed her return address in the upper left-hand corner.

On the small table in the apartment kitchenette were several romance novels that Clea had finished reading. On the spine of each was printed the name of a publishing house.

Clea turned the slim paperback books over and over in her hand. They all seemed to be published by companies located in New York.

She selected one at random, then copied down the address from the copyright page. With big, bold strokes of a marking pen she addressed the envelope: "Romance

Editor, Herald Square Publications." Thinking quickly, she crossed out her own name from the title page, and scribbled in her new pseudonym: Serena Veronese. Why not? It had a certain panache, she decided, and at least, this way, the Bottington image would have a chance of remaining intact.

Clea shut her eyes for a moment, then placed the partially completed manuscript in the envelope, which she finished addressing before stapling it shut. Satisfied, she placed the package in a brown supermarket bag so she could discreetly carry it out to the mailbox. Then she slipped a rubber band around the carbon copy of her manuscript, and slid the bundle into a drawer.

Just taking this action made her feel considerably better. Clea smiled triumphantly, amazed at her own daring. Donning her chocolate-hued Burberry raincoat and tucking her fair hair under a brown-and-green plaid tam-o'-shanter, she prepared to leave the apartment.

Outside the rain was coming down in buckets. Combining with the afternoon fog, it made the day especially dismal, even for San Francisco in midwinter.

Clea lowered her head as she descended the apartment-house steps and, once again, almost bumped into Professor Tanners, who was incongruously dressed in overalls and a red plaid shirt. He was lugging two enormous brown bags filled with what appeared to be cleaning supplies, and perhaps a few miscellaneous grocery items.

Biting back the impulse to laugh at the comical figure he cut, Clea immediately offered to help, an offer the professor clearly couldn't refuse: the sodden bags were in imminent danger of breaking.

"I'm cleaning house today," Mr. Tanners told her.

"How ambitious of you," Clea murmured as she followed him back into the apartment house, again forcing herself to stifle an irresistible bubble of laughter. Ten minutes later she reemerged from the building after having reluctantly accepted a "thank you" cup of tea.

Making her way down the steps of the lavender building for what she hoped would be the last time that day,
her head jerked in surprised recognition of the figure
descending the staircase of the apartment house next door.
Although she couldn't see his face, the man's regal bear-
ing and energetic stride were oddly familiar. But who of
her acquaintances would frequent a neighborhood like
this? She couldn't think of anyone.

Shaking her head, Clea approached the mailbox and
dropped the manuscript inside. She gave one last glance
at the figure now retreating down the street, and again
failed to connect it with any name she knew. And then,
lost in the enormity of what she had done—had she,
Clea Witherspoon Bottington, actually mailed off a torrid
romance to a publisher in New York?—she forgot all
about the encounter. It was nearly three, she noted,
checking her watch.

When she got home Kevin was already there, along
with both David and Boppo. Absently, Clea dropped her
parking ticket on top of the pile of bills to be paid on
Mitch's desk. All three little boys tried at once to explain
that there was a special early kiddy show at the movie
theater. Boppo's mother was coming to pick them up.
Could Kevin go? Huh, huh? Mrs. Brown would stay at
the movies with them too, okay? Please?

Clea had little desire to stay alone in the near-empty
house. The day servants had already gone, and even the
young maid had departed, leaving behind a hastily scribbled note of explanation, something about a sick relative.

Clea sighed. To deny a child out of her own selfish
needs wouldn't be fair, so she said, "All right."

Outside, a car honked its horn, and Clea watched her
son and his buddies disappear as if by magic. The house
was suddenly silent.

Slowly climbing the winding stairs to her bedroom,

Clea found herself wishing fervently that Mitch would make it home early as he'd promised. But when she stepped out of the shower moments later to answer the phone on its sixth ring, her hopes were dashed. It must be Mitch, calling to say he'd be late. Clutching a heavy jacquard towel around her, she wondered if her husband had caught a cold. He sounded odd.

"I'm calling from the airport," he said in a flat voice. "There's been an explosion at our chemical facility in Portland. The only plane I could get leaves in an hour. I'm sorry."

Clea sank down on a nearby chair feeling all alone in the world. She knew it was selfish, but she couldn't help it. "When will you be back?" she asked, trying to keep the forlorn note from her voice.

"Sunday if I'm lucky; Monday if I'm not." There was a perceptible pause, and then he added, "I've been calling for the last two hours. Have you been at the hairdresser's?"

"No, um, I was out shopping," she lied.

"Anything in particular?" Mitch queried. How odd for him to ask, Clea thought. He never did. He never showed the slightest interest in domestic matters.

"Oh, I was thinking of redecorating the bedroom," Clea said hastily, "and I just wanted to see what was available." There was another long pause. "Are you all right?" Clea asked finally.

"No, I'm not!" Mitch said, slamming down the phone. It was all Clea needed. Even when her husband was ill, he never admitted it. But clearly something was very wrong.

She let the towel drop to the floor, hastily grabbing a madras blouse, its brilliant woven pattern contrasting strongly with her turquoise cotton slacks. Clea slipped her bare feet into leather sandals, pulled her hair back in a ponytail, and ran downstairs.

She didn't stop for a jacket, and the realization that she hadn't put on any underwear, either, didn't hit her until she was more than ten miles from home. It didn't make any difference. Nothing did, except the fact that her husband had hung up on her, and he was definitely not all right. If Mitch needed her, she would fly to the other end of the world on wings of straw.

As Clea sped toward the airport, she thought how odd it was that writing the book, which had thrown their intimate life into such a maelstrom, had at the same time improved it so much, had brought them closer together. Until now . . . What was going on with Mitch, anyway? She pressed her foot more firmly on the gas.

When she got to the airport, Clea decided, she would make things all right for Mitch. Maybe she'd even tell him about the book. How seriously could he take it? Plenty of women wrote books. Even those married to notable men, though perhaps such women didn't write romances. But on the other hand, didn't women from all walks of life and all occupations need the spark of romance in their lives? Had she, Clea, really done anything wrong?

As she pulled the Rolls Royce into San Francisco Airport's short-term parking section, she wondered whether she'd be able to catch Mitch before he boarded that plane. The thought made her hurry. She *had* to see him. But maybe this wasn't the time to tell him about the book. She'd tell him when he returned. In the quiet of their bedroom. Now, she had to tend to him. Find out what was on his mind, why he'd slammed down the phone, whether he was sick, or what. This was no time to upset him further.

Oblivious to the stares of passersby, she sprinted across the terminal, the sweeping movement of the minute hand on the clocks she passed reminding her that the plane was probably already in the process of loading.

But her luck held. There had been a delay in the plane's arrival, and in addition, a computer error had resulted in apparent overbooking. Hence the boarding line was long and slow-moving.

She spotted Mitch near the end of it. He was carrying his briefcase and the small suitcase he kept in the office for travel emergencies. She called his name, loud enough to be heard above the hubbub, and though he spun around, he seemed so lost in his own thoughts that he almost failed to recognize her.

But then, Clea didn't look much like herself. In the vivid madras blouse, with the airport lights outlining her full, loose breasts, and her pale hair pulled back off her face, she looked more like a college student, knapsack hidden somewhere under a chair, than a Bottington matron.

Mitch stared at her with something approaching agony, a pain he seemed to be trying hard to conceal but couldn't quite manage. He moved toward her, slowly, as if he didn't quite know what to say or do.

Interpreting this as evidence of some grave malady, Clea hurled herself at him. She threw her arms around his neck and pulled his face down to hers. His arm went around her waist, holding her against him as if by doing so he could shield them from all harm.

"Mitch, I was so terrified," Clea said, tears rolling down her cheeks. "I thought you'd been hurt. I thought someone at the plant had been killed, and that you were blaming yourself. I thought... Oh, I don't know what I thought. I just had to see for myself that you were all right."

As she talked, she moved away from him slightly, then noticed the ashen pallor and the slight dark stubble

on his face. Hadn't he even bothered to shave before
leaving the office? "You *are* all right?" she asked hesitantly, fear drumming at her temples, a hideous knot
forming in her stomach.

"Do you really care?" he asked, gazing at her with
such pain and sadness that words almost failed her. She
gave him a penetrating look before saying earnestly, "Of
course I care. Of course I do. Do you think I rushed here
like a madwoman because I hadn't received my quota of
speeding tickets for the year?"

Clea realized she sounded hysterical, but what kind
of a question was that? It made no sense. Whatever
arguments she'd had with Mitch over the years, and there
had been many, she had always cared. Maybe too much
for her own good.

But if the question made no sense, neither did her
husband's subsequent remark, blurted out just as the
boarding line finally began to move in earnest. The loudspeaker blared an announcement of the plane's imminent
departure.

"It will be easy enough to find out if that's true," he
said, moving his index finger over her aquiline nose,
then tracing the outlines of her mouth, as if trying to
commit both to memory. "Mistakes in identity are com-
mon. Even among people with twenty-twenty vision."

With that he kissed Clea on her forehead, spun around,
and strode off, catching up with the line as it disappeared
through the door to the loading ramp.

Feeling as though she had been hit by a mallet, Clea
tried to understand. Mistaken identity? Twenty-twenty
vision? What did he mean by that?

For some reason the image of her neglected hairdresser
popped unbidden into her mind. How long had it been
since she'd seen him? Ardenne wore contact lenses, which
he was always misplacing. Being too vain to wear glasses,

he could be a positive menace at times. Especially with a scissors. Clea had learned to peer deeply into his eyes to check for the telltale edges of the plastic discs.

The thought made her smile even now, the upturned corners of her mouth an odd contrast to the puzzled frown still on her brow. Was it possible that her husband was going through what was euphemistically termed "male menopause"?

No, she decided. At thirty-three he was entirely too young. Besides, Mitch wasn't the emotional type. The only time she'd seen him lose his composure was during lovemaking. Especially lately.

Clea stopped, bought herself a lukewarm hot dog, slathered it with taste-concealing mustard, put a quarter in the newspaper vending machine, and lowered herself into one of the waiting-room chairs.

It was perhaps mere chance that today's San Francisco *Chronicle* contained a feature on how to inflate a husband's ego when business pressures get him down. Another odd coincidence was the blurb Clea caught in the social column. "Mitchell Bottington, high-powered president of Klectronics International, still manages to find time to participate in activities at the school attended by his seven-year-old son, Kevin. Bottington recently took on the presidency of the Parent-Teacher Liaison Group. Asked about the rapidly escalating controversy on library book censorship, his response was, 'We'll make sure that our children use their study time to read American history, not American garbage.'"

Didn't that sound just like her husband! More P.R. for Klectronics!

Still, the mention of Mitch's "high-powered" job combined in her thoughts with the earlier article on overworked husbands, and the wheels of Clea's brain began to spin.

Throughout the leisurely drive home she explored first one alternative, then another. Clearly Mitch was working too hard; he needed cheering up. But she hadn't the remotest idea of how to accomplish this, she thought ruefully, the iron gates of Hampstead Estates clicking behind her.

It was only as she made her way through the bedroom and into the bathroom to prepare for her shower that Clea recalled Tony Bernardo's mirror-plated abode.

A plush towel wrapped around her slim frame, she strolled around the large bedroom, taking in curtains, carpet, wallpaper, even the fixtures. She had always thought of the bedroom she shared with Mitch as a study in restrained elegance. But now, suddenly, it seemed just plain dull.

Clea was still humming cheerfully when Kevin reappeared. "Where's Daddy?" he asked, clutching the remains of an uneaten carton of popcorn from the movie theater. It was a sure sign he wouldn't have room for dinner.

"Business, business, and more business," Clea replied, giving her son an affectionate hug.

"Again?" the child chirped, looking somewhat downcast. "I was just getting used to him being around. How long will he be gone this time?"

"Just till Monday. That's not really very long. Besides, I need your help on a secret project."

Kevin's cherubic face perked up immediately. "What secret project?"

"I am going to redecorate Daddy's and my bedroom while he's gone. I want to brighten it up. Would you like to come shopping with me? You can help me pick everything out."

"What do you mean, 'brighten it up'?" Kevin asked suspiciously.

"I was thinking in terms of red and white, mostly," Clea replied, a touch of conspiratorial mischief in her voice.

"Daddy will hate it," the seven-year-old bluntly informed her.

"I'll buy you a giant-size chocolate bar," Clea bribed.

"If you'll make it with nuts, you've got a deal," Kevin replied. He'd apparently inherited his corporate negotiation style from his father.

Clea laughed and hugged him again. Picking up the phone, she made a few calls. In less than an hour, and for a quite sizeable sum to anyone other than a Bottington, she had made arrangements to have the bedroom ceiling covered with mirrored tiles by the following night.

And that was only the beginning. By midafternoon the following day, Clea had purchased white satin sheets, heart-embroidered white satin pillowcases, and a very plush red velvet bedspread. All for the round king-sized bed that arrived, as requested, just before four-thirty.

By five-thirty the bedroom was festooned with such a quantity of trailing plants that it was beginning to resemble the Amazon jungle. An hour later three enormous boxes containing black and white mock-zebra pillows had arrived by special messenger. And by eight o'clock the last of the workmen had gone; the ceiling was finished.

The only items still lacking were two red velvet chairs and two gilded cupid lamps. These arrived by noon on Sunday.

"How does it look?" Clea asked, as Kevin peered around the room, wide-eyed.

"I sure hope you know what you're doing, Mom," was his only reply.

"Of course I know what I'm doing," Clea said. And she was quite sure she did—until she settled down in the newly decorated room for a well-deserved rest.

Clea was all set to snuggle down in the satin sheets, but they were disconcertingly slippery. Worse than that, the massive trailing greenery created eerie shadows on the wall that danced before her closed eyelids and jarred her from her brief attempts at sleep. And every time she opened her eyes to look at the ceiling, she found herself confronted by distorted images of her baggy-eyed, sleep-deprived self.

She finally gave up. Traipsing into the guest bedroom, she at last found welcome sleep. She wasn't sure what time the next day Mitch would arrive, but she couldn't greet him with dark circles under her eyes. Of course, with any luck the bedroom would seem more functional when Mitch was in it with her. She sincerely hoped so.

With that thought drifting through her mind, Clea's dreams were relatively mellow.

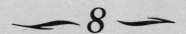

8

MITCH ARRIVED HOME the following morning just as Clea was about to depart for her journalistic hideaway.

"Leaving?" he asked tonelessly, by way of greeting. Clea, who had been about to run to him, stopped in her tracks.

"Well, I was. But I guess I'm not," she replied, rooted to the spot. Mitch looked as if he hadn't slept in three days. His face was gaunt and weary, and his impenetrable slate eyes were surrounded by dark circles.

"Do you have an appointment with the hairdresser? A fashion show? A committee meeting? By all means, don't let me keep you."

As Mitch scrutinized her intently, Clea felt distinctly ill at ease. It was as though there were a solid wall between them, albeit an invisible one.

"Will you please tell me what on earth happened in Portland?" Clea asked. "You're looking at me as if I were part of the enemy camp. So why don't you either shoot me and put me out of my misery, or inform me of truce terms."

Mitch put his coat on the hall coat rack. Turning his back to her, he walked into the living room and poured himself a full glass of whiskey. He downed it in two gulps.

"Nothing much happened in Portland," he replied, staring at the curtains floating in the window, his back still toward her.

Walking up to him, Clea put her hand on his shoulder. Then, resting her head between his shoulder blades, she allowed her arms to drift around his waist.

"I missed you," she said softly.

"Did you?"

"Yes. Is it some kind of crime to miss one's husband?" Clea asked with more than a touch of annoyance.

"No. But I am gone so often . . ."

Clea dropped her hands immediately. Stepping around to face him, she put a cool hand to his forehead, testing for fever. Her husband was always very quick to deny the frequency of his absences. Was she hearing things?

Mitch stared down at her. Placing his strong hands gently on her head, he moved them down over her eyes, her nose, her mouth, her throat, then out across her shoulders, where they remained, resting lightly.

"Clea . . ." he began. She looked up at him questioningly. "Clea . . ." he began again. His broad shoulders seemed to slump. "Oh, what the hell. Forget it."

"Forget what?" There seemed to be some kind of war being fought inside her husband. It was as though there were something he wanted to say, yet was terribly afraid to say.

"Forget what?" she repeated.

"Nothing." He shrugged. "Anyhow, I've got to take

a shower and get over to the office. We'll talk about it later, okay?"

It was certainly not okay. But Clea knew from past experience that when her husband was ready to discuss something, he would. Until then, you couldn't pry it out of him with a crowbar.

"Okay," she said sulkily. She picked up a magazine, pretending to scan its colorful pages. She heard Mitch walk out of the living room, down the hallway, and up the stairs.

"Oh, my god!" His voice echoed down to the living room.

Suddenly a vision of the redecorated bedroom flashed across Clea's mind. She had completely forgotten about that!

Taking the stairs two at a time, she entered the room to find Mitch staring fixedly at the mirrored ceiling, holding one of the mock-zebra pillows by its tassel as if it were a skunk. And, whatever reaction she had expected, it wasn't the fantastically happy grin now spreading from ear to ear across his face.

"You actually *were* shopping for bedroom furnishings," he said, as if such an excursion were a gift from the saints.

Clea looked at him quizzically. "Of course I was shopping," she said, watching him wander around the room, the expression on his face reminiscent of a kid in candyland. "I mean, you don't find these gilt cupid lamps growing on bushes, do you?"

The cupid lamps in question, when seen in the starkness of morning light, looked incredibly tawdry. "Marvelous lamps," Mitch exclaimed, patting them affectionately before parking his six-foot frame in one of the entirely too small red velvet chairs. "Great chair," he praised.

The brilliant red and white of the room made Clea want to shut her eyes and refocus. What ever had inspired her to choose a color scheme capable of producing an instant migraine?

"I'll get rid of it tomorrow," she promised hesitantly, still waiting for the ultraconservative Mitchell Eduard Bottington to tell her to do it all over in blacks and browns.

"Great bedroom," Mitch said, rising from the chair. He lay down on the bed, staring up at his fully-clothed recumbent figure in the mirrored tiles above. He looked ten years younger than he had ten minutes ago.

"You actually like it?" Clea asked in disbelief.

Mitch waved to his reflection in the mirror. "Great mirror," he said.

Clea sat down on one of the red velvet chairs. It was as comfortable as a rock. A small spider crawled merrily up the split-leaf philodendron. She supposed the florist had charged her for that, too. She wondered what other creatures were thriving in the rest of the massive pots. "Great plants," Mitch enthused as if in response to her thoughts.

"Wonderful." Clea sighed, thinking that never in her wildest dreams could she have anticipated such a positive response from Mitch.

"Aren't you going to come sit by my side? " Mitch asked with a teasing smile. "Or are you afraid of what you'll see in the mirror?"

"I'll see one loony female Bottington next to one loony male Bottington," she replied, quite certain she spoke the truth. But what she saw, as she slowly complied with his request, was her handsome husband lovingly kissing her fingertips, one by one.

"Oh," she said, tiny electrical charges racing down her spine. "Oh," she giggled, as Mitch duplicated the procedure, this time licking the tips of her fingers as well.

Warming to his task, he then went on to kiss the tip of her nose, her eyelids, her earlobes, her chin, and every other portion of Clea that wasn't covered by her pale peach V-neck angora sweater and linen slacks. It was all so delightful.

"Did you buy a red and white valentine nightgown to go with the bedroom?" Mitch asked deadpan, pulling her sweater up slightly to kiss her navel.

"You mean one of those things you told me I'd catch pneumonia in?" Clea responded as Mitch blew softly into her belly button.

"Can't catch pneumonia with a man like me around," he countered, sounding almost exactly as he had during their courting days, when he'd suggested a midnight skinny dip in a friend's pool. "Which reminds me," he added, circling the angora-covered peaks of her breasts with his fingertips, "you ought to do something about your clothes. They don't color-coordinate with the room."

My clothes don't color-coordinate with the room, Clea thought. My husband wants me to wear a valentine nightie. He returned home from a business trip in the foulest mood I've ever seen, and as soon as he caught sight of my decorating job, he became as cheerful as a bee in spring. That magazine was right!

Clea was abruptly brought back to the present as Mitch began sliding her slacks down over her hips. She watched him in the mirror. He wasn't making a very efficient job of it, for he kept interrupting his progress to kiss every newly bared inch.

Moments later, however, she found herself peering up at a naked lady reposing on a scarlet bedspread under the admiring gaze of a gentleman impeccably clad in a three-piece suit.

"This is embarrassing," Clea remarked. But why? she thought. Maybe it was the mirrors. They made everything seem so public. She crawled under the covers.

"Not fair," Mitch chided.

"But it's chilly," Clea fibbed.

"I'll take care of that in a minute," Mitch promised with gusto.

He was as good as his vow. Draping one warm and slightly fuzzy leg over Clea's body, he began to draw intricate designs on bare flesh with an unexpectedly talented tongue. Every so often he would peer solemnly at the invisible results of his etchings and murmur, "I hope you realize this one's a pear," or "Did you notice that this one's a pomegranate?"

Clea was noticing nothing. She had passed into a state of contented oblivion and was quite content to lay there motionless.

"Turn over," Mitch commanded.

"But then I can't see myself," Clea whispered almost drowsily.

"You've got your eyes closed anyhow," Mitch observed, and Clea wriggled obediently onto her stomach. Mitch resumed his titillating tracings, this time focusing on the outermost portion of her thigh.

It took her at least five minutes to discover he was no longer using his tongue to design the peaches, plums, and kumquats he kept announcing with such award-winning pride. But the new sensation was so tender, so silken, she was hardly about to protest.

Clea's nails dug into the bedspread as she forced herself to remain still. It was so nice, so very nice, being the totally passive recipient of her husband's attentions. It's not that she didn't enjoy the aggressive techniques she had employed these last few weeks; it was just . . . it was just . . .

She hadn't expected Mitch to enter her yet, and the

sudden demand of his ramrod hardness gave her a start. But then, as the intruder eased its way into her moist, heated flesh, she started to shift position slightly.

"Don't move," Mitch gasped. "Please, don't move. This particular work of art is going to be entirely my creation."

And it was exactly that. As Clea moaned, begging for relief, Mitch controlled her every response. He made her whimper. He made her plead.

"Damn you," she cried, and with that, Mitch filled her entire body with the shooting flame of his own desire.

Later, as they lay exhausted between the sheets, Mitch's head resting on the embroidered satin pillow, Clea's nestled in the hollow of his shoulder, she found herself thinking lusciously of his welcome dominance.

When Clea awoke, minutes or hours later—she wasn't sure which—she was all alone. Groggily, she rose from the bed, feeling as if every bone had turned to rubber, and headed straight for the shower.

When she emerged from the bathroom, wearing lounging pajamas, Mitch was hoisting an exuberant Kevin onto his shoulder. Kevin was shouting "Giddy-app horsey" with such glee that Clea could barely hear herself think.

"You're terribly quiet," Mitch said, interrupting her thoughts.

Clea realized she had been staring into empty space. Kevin had gone and she could hear the television blaring. Mitch was watching her closely. Husbands had no right to be that handsome, Clea thought.

She observed the laugh crinkles around his slate-gray eyes, the funny little forelock that he had been trying—unsuccessfully—to tame since he was a teenager, the way his nose appeared to be perfectly straight until you discovered the now-subtle effects of an old football injury.

Mitch had barely aged since the first day Clea had met him. That was the best thing about a good marriage: for some reason your mate continued to look as lovely as on the day you fell in love.

"Am I just as pretty as I was when you met me?" Clea asked dreamily.

The question seemed to catch Mitch off guard. But he recovered quickly. "The day I met you," he said, "you were a pretty little girl pretending to be grown up. Now you're a woman, and a hundred times more beautiful."

Clea felt a flush of pleasure at the rare compliment. "Mitch, there's something I want to tell you," she said, determined to confess her secret literary life to him despite the trembling in her knees.

"Later," Mitch interrupted. "I have something I want to show you first."

"It's important," she insisted.

"Not as important as this," he countered, taking a small, black velvet box from his pocket and handing it to her.

Clea opened the box slowly, her ivory skin pale in the lamplight. And then her breathing seemed almost to stop.

Nestled on a bed of cream satin were two of the most exquisite teardrop emerald earrings Clea had ever seen. Each was surrounded by tiny diamonds, which caught the light from the overhead lamp and scattered it across her hands.

"Put them on," Mitch requested softly. They were on arched 18-karat gold inserts, and when Clea's fingers started shaking, he did the job for her.

"A thousand times more beautiful," Mitch said, gazing directly into changeable hazel eyes that had now picked up the emerald hue.

In the end, she didn't manage to tell Mitch about her book that night. The subject completely slipped her mind as he kissed her forehead, tilted her face up toward his, and bent over to kiss her ever so lightly on the lips. It was as though she were a jewel even more precious than the ones he had just given her.

The next morning she stretched like a contented kitten, turned over to cuddle against him, and groaned with disappointment when she discovered he had already left for work.

It didn't matter now. She knew he would be home. As soon as he could make it. Because he wanted to be home. Because he wanted to be with her.

Clea wondered if she had ever been so happy. Even the garish valentine bedroom looked slightly better today. Not much better, though. She would arrange to have it redecorated immediately.

She got up and selected her outfit with care. A Gallanos silk would do: a shimmering viridian with slim tie waist, blouson top, and a flowing skirt. She caught her hair back off her forehead, pinned it loosely, and let it fall onto her shoulders, a perfect frame for the emerald earrings she now fastened in place.

Impulsively, she picked up the phone.

"This is Mrs. Bottington," she said confidently. "May I speak to my husband?"

The silence that followed was deadly. "Hello, Miss Hoven, are you still there?" Clea asked with more impatience than concern.

"Certainly," came the clipped response. "But your husband has gone out for the morning. He had some business to take care of."

"Tell my husband I'd like to have lunch with him," Clea instructed.

"I'll tell him if he gets back," Miss Hoven snapped, before slamming down the receiver.

Furious, Clea decided she would write the woman's dismissal notice herself. But then she deliberately cleared her mind of all unpleasant thoughts and finished dressing. After adding a dab of her "tempt-a-monk" perfume, she donned a lightweight brown tweed coat and checked to see if the Bottington image could be improved upon. It couldn't.

Clea glanced at her watch, then decided to make an impromptu visit to her apartment. Just because she'd mailed off the first half of her book was no reason to stop writing.

The streets around the apartment house were deserted. Quickly, Clea climbed the stairs and threw open the door.

"Our heroine returns," Mitch said dryly, his voice barbed with disgust.

Clea's mouth dropped. Before her stood her husband, holding her carbon-copied manuscript in his hands. Tearing page 1 to shreds, then balling it up, he threw it across the room, aiming for her small wastebasket. Then he picked up another sheet.

Not sure how to react, Clea bought time. She turned, locked the door behind her, walked to the kitchenette, and put on a pot of coffee, all the while listening to the insistent thud of paper hitting metal.

"I tried to tell you," she said quietly as her busy fingers laid out a cheese wedge, a few apple slices, and a fan of crackers. Anything to avoid looking at him.

"I must have missed it," Mitch snarled, dropping the rest of the manuscript into the basket with a loud plop, and seating himself in the room's one armchair, elbows on knees, face an iron mask.

"I must have said a hundred times, a thousand times, that I was lonely, that I was bored, that I felt useless."

"Well, you certainly seem to have taken care of that," Mitch snapped, studying his hands as if the whitened knuckles would provide a solution to the problem.

"Have I really done anything so awful?" She had expected Mitch to be angry, to yell or scream. But instead he just sat there, examining his hands, turning them first one way, then another.

"I guess it depends on your point of view."

Clea's expression lightened instantaneously. "I knew you'd understand. I just knew it. And I'm almost finished. It really won't take me much longer."

Mitch shot from the chair as if he had been catapulted. "No," he said, his face white with barely controlled fury. "If you try it, I'll kill you."

"What?" she gasped.

"We're not going to discuss this any further," he said adamantly.

"Why not?"

"Because there's nothing to discuss. This whole thing didn't happen. You'll close down this apartment. We'll go about our daily affairs, just as we used to. Maybe we'll get some marriage counseling. We'll work it out. For Kevin's sake, if nothing else."

"Mitchell Eduard Bottington, you are being a total ass."

"Tell me about it," he said bitterly, glaring at his impeccably clad, impeccably bred wife. "Or rather, let me tell you."

From his pants pocket he took two carefully folded sheets of white paper. He opened the first one and turned it toward her. It read *Secret Diary of Delights* by Clea Witherspoon Bottington. It was her original title sheet, the one she had discarded before submitting her book under the pseudonym Serena Veronese. "So what?" she commented.

Without replying, Mitch opened the second sheet. "I decided to save this one," he told her. He began to read it slowly. Peering over his shoulder, Clea immediately recognized it as the sensuous scene between Tanya and Tony that took place after their big fight in that tawdry red and white bedroom.

"That's the scene I threw out because it didn't seem right," Clea explained.

"So you came home, practiced on me, then came back here and did it again," Mitch remarked sardonically.

"No," Clea corrected. "I did it again here until it was as good as it could get, and then I came home and did it just for fun."

She thought she saw Mitch flinch. Without responding, he meticulously folded the pages as if they were the last pieces of paper in the world and each fold was of momentous importance.

"It's amazing," he said finally, "how we just see what we want to see. Just one question, and I won't ask any more. Does this fellow have a name?"

"Tony Bernardo. It's there on the piece of paper, remember?"

"Well, you called yourself Tanya, so I just wondered whether this construction worker, this 'Tony,' might have a real name, too. Not that it's any of my business, of course."

Mitch was trying his best to appear as if it made no difference to him, not really. But what Clea found most puzzling was the way he kept looking at her as though she were a prized orchid that had suddenly turned into a Venus flytrap.

"Tony Bernardo," she reiterated. "He's my macho man, rapidly in the process of becoming more egalitarian in his views." She said it proudly, as if it were truly a hard-won accomplishment. And then a new thought occurred to her and her face turned whiter than the sheets of paper Mitch still held.

"Mitch, are we talking about the same thing?" she asked hesitantly, a horrible realization slamming down on her like a mallet.

"Unless one of us is discoursing on the weather, I

think so," Mitch replied bitterly.

"Tanya isn't me," Clea explained. "Tanya is the heroine of my book. Mitch, that was a book manuscript you threw away, not a real diary. Tony is Tanya's boyfriend. They're fictional characters. I made them up out of my head. Neither of them exists. Honest."

"Then what about this?" Mitch queried in disgust, as he strode to Clea's small desk, pulled open a bottom drawer, and began throwing out her graphic sex manuals and magazines as if they were pitch-pennies. Some of them landed spread-eagled on the floor. Clea winced.

"That's my research," she said, staring at a photo of one particularly convoluted scene. Mitch was staring at it too. She watched the familiar blush creep over his white shirt collar. For a change, she agreed. She bent down and flipped the magazine shut. "At least it's part of my research," she added.

Her husband still seemed skeptical. "I'm writing a romance," Clea blurted, trying to get the whole affair into perspective.

"A what?" Mitch asked, glancing from his wife to the small print text he was holding and back again. Clea recalled purchasing that particular volume at a used-book store. She had read just three pages before burying it at the bottom of her review stack.

"A romance," Clea replied, feeling somewhat foolish. She started to explain, but the more she explained, the worse it all sounded. She began to wish there was a sandpile nearby and that she was an ostrich and could at least make her head disappear from view. Make that a magician and her entire self.

And then Mitch started to laugh. At first it was a little laugh, more like an entry-level chuckle. This increased in volume until the small room practically shook from the sound.

Clea started to laugh too, as much from relief as from anything else. And then she stopped short and asked, "What's so funny?"

"Me. You. Us. For days I've been tearing myself apart thinking you were having an affair with some bearded fellow in this building. All the while I was in Portland, running around from one meeting to another trying to calm everybody down, I kept wondering whether you were going to be there when I got back. At the same time, of course, I kept assuring myself you were totally incapable of nefarious conduct and I was acting like a jealous fool. You don't know how relieved I was to see the fluorescent tinsel bedroom. When you said you were redecorating the bedroom, I'd assumed that was just another excuse to account for your time."

"What? How dare you think me capable of adultery!" Clea said furiously.

Mitch tried to interrupt, but Clea angrily told him to keep quiet, she wasn't finished talking. With a rather astonished expression on his face, he kept quiet.

Clea continued. "Nor do I appreciate your spying on me, and last but not least, who let you into my apartment?"

Letting five seconds elapse for safety before he replied, Mitch responded with, "Your landlord let me in. I explained that you were my wife and that you had inadvertently left our plane tickets inside. Your landlord is a very understanding man."

"How much did it take to bribe him?" Clea inquired.

"Bribery is an ugly term," Mitch responded with the nonchalance of someone who has carried out this type of transaction many, many times. "I merely gave him your Christmas present in advance. A mere pittance, I assure you."

"A mere pittance," Clea reiterated. "Of course. And how did you find out about my apartment?"

"Sheer coincidence, not spying. Paul Caroters, your long-term admirer, was visiting an elderly aunt who lives near here. He saw you enter the building with a dark, bearded man in workman's overalls, and he didn't see you come out. So he did his civic duty and called me."

"And of course, without any facts to support his accusation, you decided I was cheating on you."

"No," Mitch replied, looking very self-righteous, even for Mitch. "I merely entered it into the stream of my consciousness, which unfortunately was somewhat distracted due to the Portland incident. But I did ask what you had been doing that day, remember?"

"Oh," Clea said slowly, her memory bank blipping up the pre-airport telephone call. "That's when I told you about my boudoir restyling."

"Precisely. And I *might* have let the entire matter rest, except Miss Hoven found your parking ticket in a pile of bills. I couldn't help but notice that it showed your car to have been in the self-same neighborhood in which Caroters claimed to have seen you."

Clea didn't want to hear any more. She knew the rest. "I think you and I had better go have lunch and a couple of dry martinis," she invited. "I've had enough for one morning."

"A woman after my own stomach." Mitch smiled gratefully. "Also my heart, as soon as my stomach is taken care of." He made a pretend bow, then offered his arm gallantly.

With the regalness of a duchess accepting the favors of a duke, Clea linked her arm through his. Actually she felt more like a princess, or even a queen, resplendent in emeralds and silk. How petty she had been to think Mitch would be angry about her novel. She would have to apologize later, for he had accepted it with perfect understanding.

Mitch held the door open for her and Clea looked

fondly back over her shoulder at this sanctuary she could now share with her husband.

Seeing her look back, Mitch kissed her fondly on the forehead. "Don't worry about this mess," he remarked generously. "I'll have someone come in and clean it out."

"What did you say?" Clea asked disbelievingly. A cold draft came in through the open door and slapped her in the face.

"I said don't worry about this place," Mitch repeated authoritatively. "I'm sure the landlord, upon proper consideration, won't give us a hard time about breaking the lease. And I'll pay some salvage group to come in here and cart away all this junk. You won't have to bother with anything."

Clea was still standing by the open door. She didn't even feel the chill anymore. "This isn't junk," she enunciated icily. "It's material I need to finish my book."

"What book?"

Taking a slow, deep breath, Clea let it out one word at a time: "The romance novel I'm writing."

"Oh, that," Mitch said with a tidy gesture of dismissal.

"Oh, that, what?" Clea asked, her hazel eyes narrowed into slits and her jaw stubbornly set.

"Oh, that piece of garbage," Mitch stated forthrightly.

It was like turning up the flame under a simmering pot. "For your information, the first half of 'that piece of garbage' is out at a publisher's right now," Clea shot back, her anger boiling over. "I have such faith in it that I fully intend to send along the second half before too long."

"No," Mitch said flatly, closing the apartment door and standing with his back to it as a barrier. "No, you will not finish the second half, and yes, you will request that the first half be returned."

"Any particular reason?" Clea inquired frostily, crossing her arms in front of her shimmering silk-covered chest.

"Because there's always a chance, however slim, that someone might decide to publish it, and——"

"And that would tarnish the Bottington image," Clea interrupted, completing the explanation for him.

"It would more than tarnish the Bottington image; it would make me a laughingstock. Especially since I've taken on the P.T.L.G. presidency. Now that I'm officially on record as opposing obscene books."

"My book is not obscene," Clea denied vehemently. When Mitch's reply was silence, she sizzled. "I suppose you would have preferred to discover I *was* having an affair?"

"Among those who share the Bottington genealogy, I am certain there are some who have had affairs. But"—and he paused deliberately to make certain she got the uncompromising message—"there isn't one who has written a public proclamation of his most intimate . . . fantasies." He cleared his throat.

"Mitch!" Clea cried, hoping for a straw of understanding, yet wanting to throw a chair at him with full force. "Mitch, it's a romance. It's a story. It's an entertainment. The erotic scenes are only a very small part of the book."

"No," he commanded, sounding for all the world like some five-star general ordering a mere private about.

"Yes," she countermanded insolently, turning her back on him. Walking to her desk, she took out a sheet of paper and slipped it efficiently into her typewriter. She began to type furiously, hammering out word after word in the tense silence. If Mitch had looked over her shoulder, he would have seen paragraphs from the Gettysburg Address, which Clea had been forced to memorize in a long-ago history class. But he didn't look.

"The P.T.L.G. book debate is scheduled to take place

three weeks from now," he pronounced, opening the apartment door. "Your tenancy in this apartment will end tonight. Let me know when you decide what to do."

With that he slammed the door behind him. Clea glanced down at the sentence she had been typing: ". . . and that government of the people, by the people, for the people, shall not perish from the earth."

Too bad he hadn't given her a chance to fling it at him, Clea thought. Somewhere, sometime, someplace, somebody has to call a stop and say "We won't knuckle under any more."

Outside the parameters of her rectangular apartment window the sky was almost a periwinkle blue, so bright and clean it might have been newly washed and polished. In the farthest reaches one lone cloud drifted by, a maverick in an otherwise cloudless day.

Clea tracked it, tears streaming down her face, their glistening brilliance a perfect complement to the emerald earrings with their unfathomable depths set off by diamond purity. She reached into her purse, made a few futile swipes at her cheeks and chin with a crumpled tissue, then did a quite un-Bottingtonlike thing and blew her nose noisily.

The honking sound, there in that drab apartment occupied only by a slim, aristocratic blonde perched behind a typewriter, fingers still on the keys, and a random scattering of erotic literature creating flesh-toned flashes on the floor, seemed to suggest that somebody long out of practice had taken up the saxophone. It was so incongruous that, despite herself, Clea smiled. It was a rather wan smile, more an attempt at a smile than an actual smile. But it broke her dejection.

"Goodness, me, Mitchell Bottington," she said to the cloud which had now reached mid-window in its meanderings. "I suppose that even with two people who love each other very much, as we do, there are going to be some very trying periods. And this, my darling husband, is one of them."

She honked into the tissue again. Romance heroines never were so fallible. Their noses turned up merrily, were often touched by the merest smattering of freckles, and were always meant to be kissed. When they cried, even cried buckets, their eyes might shimmer with dewdrops but their sinuses would never plug up. Oh well, she thought, rising from her seat and checking her swollen-lidded reflection in the dull mirror of the tiny bathroom, I guess I'll have to pass on being a heroine. I'll leave that to Tanya. I'm just the writer.

And how she would write! She vowed that she would go way beyond round beds and mahogany table tops. Tanya and Tony would find sensuous delight in swimming pools, forest groves, maybe even construction sites, and bulldozer seats . . . the possibilities were endless. Did she even need Mitch anymore? With the aid of a few more reference books, she was willing to bet that she'd be able to create the gourmet meal without the help of a co-chef.

In her viridian silk dress and color-coordinated slingback spike-heeled shoes, Clea exited the apartment. She walked down the hall, descended the back stairway, and entered the area marked by a placard instructing tenants to PLEASE BAG YOUR TRASH.

Congratulating herself on finding three apparently immaculate cartons among the debris, she returned to her "sanctuary" to pack. There was no point in defying her husband on the issue of the apartment. Clea had no doubt that Mitch would simply bribe the landlord and have her evicted on some pretext or another. But if Mitch thought that was going to stop her from writing, he had another thing coming.

After packing her research books and magazines in the cartons, she carried them, one by one, out to the car.

When she emerged with the typewriter, Professor Tanners caught her in the hall. "Are you leaving us?" he asked with polite curiosity.

"I'm going home," Clea responded, weary but adamant.

"Was that your husband I saw coming out of here earlier? He looked quite angry."

Clea's mouth set into a stubborn line, and her wide hazel eyes flashed with determination. "Yes, that was my husband," she said. "But right now I don't think he's very happy about that fact," she added, an ironic edge to her voice.

"Why not, if it's not too presumptuous of me to ask?"

"Because he doesn't want his wife to be anything but a decorative adjunct to him," Clea sputtered, her anger getting the best of her.

"An intelligent woman never ages, only grows more beautiful," Professor Tanners observed wistfully. "I'm a widower, myself. Elsa had a doctorate in philosophy. I miss dear Elsa ferociously," he added.

"I'm sorry," Clea said sympathetically, but her thoughts were already off elsewhere.

Within an hour and a half from the time Mitch stormed out of her apartment, Clea had turned in the key to the landlord, and half an hour later she was carting the first of her research material up the stairs of the palatial Bottington mansion.

Clea dumped the box unceremoniously on the red velvet bedspread of her brilliant bedroom. "Goodness me, Mitchell Bottington," she said out loud to the empty bedroom, kicking off her shoes and bouncing on the bed next to her scurrilous package. "I hope you like sleeping next to the competition."

On her third trip out to the car, she was accosted by the maid, who handed her a neatly printed message. It was from Mrs. DomPeter, asking for written confirmation that Clea would appear at the P.T.L.G. debate three weeks hence.

It was the first item Clea typed on her transported typewriter. "Dear Mrs. DomPeter," she wrote. "You may be assured I will attend. Sincerely, Clea Bottington."

As she licked the envelope flap, Clea's smile was more mischievous than malicious. She had a lot of work to do in three weeks.

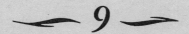

9

IT SEEMED MORE like three years. Clea didn't say anything when Mitch had the handyman bring a folding twin bed and set it up in Kevin's room. She could understand his determination to sleep separately, but why he wanted to stay with Kevin and not in one of the myriad guest rooms, she couldn't fathom. Clea reflected that it was probably because he was unaccustomed to sleeping alone. Similarly, she said nothing when Mitch removed the pile of stock market reports, the half-read murder mystery, and the alarm clock that played "Waltzing Matilda" from their bedside table. She even managed to keep quiet when he made his thirtieth reappearance in the room, this time to retrieve the back scrubber from its normal perch in the recess of the tub. But when he strode in at 11 P.M. as purposefully as if he were going to war, only to remove the toothpaste, Clea raised her voice in protest.

"Isn't this getting rather childish?" she asked scorn-

fully. A pale figure clad in brown velvet with her hair
in a ponytail, she seemed totally out of place in the tawdry
bedroom.

"*I* am not the one being childish," he emphasized with
equal scorn. "I am merely asserting my rights as the man
and wage earner of this house."

"You sound like Tony at the beginning of my book.
Before he saw the error of his ways, of course."

"Who's Tony?"

"My hero."

"Is he married to a woman who writes pornographic
literature?"

"He's not married."

"Well, then he's my hero too." And with that, Mitch
took her favorite soft pillow from the bed, deliberately
checked to see if there was anything else he had forgotten
that might add to the evening's comfort, then nodded
toward her typewriter perched on the table, but not to
Clea, and said "Good night."

Clea threw the remaining pillows, including the mock-
zebra ones, across the room. She lay down on her back
on the bed. Every time she opened her eyes she saw
herself reflected in the ceiling mirrors. Worse than that,
she saw the red velvet bedspread.

She got up, pulled off the spread, and dumped it in
the corner on top of the pillows. The gilded cupids on
the lamps seemed to have developed real eyes, which
were following her every action. From the drawer she
took two filmy nightgowns and wound them around the
lamps. "So you don't catch pneumonia," she said to no
one in particular.

Quiet, quiet, quiet. Lord, it was quiet. Ever so stealth-
ily she opened the door. On bare feet she tiptoed down
the hall, pausing before the door to Kevin's room.

"Why are you sleeping in here, Daddy?" she heard
Kevin ask groggily.

"Your mother and I are having an argument," Mitch·
responded honestly.

"Is it going to last long?" Kevin inquired, sounding
slightly concerned. "Boppo and I once had an argument
and it lasted two whole days. I got very lonesome."

"I don't think this one is going to last long," Mitch
said with a yawn. "Your mother will get lonesome too,
and she'll come around to my way of thinking."

Why, that male chauvinist blockhead! Clea fumed,
barely resisting the urge to pound on Kevin's door with
her fists. Her resistance was lowered even further when
Kevin asked, with childish wisdom, "How do you know
your way of thinking is the right way?"

It was mild insubordination, but it evoked no discernibly audible reaction from Mitch. There was a moment's hesitation, but only a moment's, before he said,
"I am absolutely correct in this matter. Now go to sleep."

Silence. More silence. Clea's smoldering rage was
becoming white hot. He could at least have made an
effort to understand what her writing meant to his wife.
He could have at least asked her what the plot was about.
He could even, in a moment of supreme generosity, have
offered to read the book so he could make a fair judgment.

But no. He would just condemn it. Her husband, for
all intents and purposes, was no better than Mrs.
DomPeter. In fact, he should have married Mrs.
DomPeter. They could be virtuous together, bedding down
on opposite sides of the world with two hundred cats in
between.

The more Clea thought about it, the angrier she got.
Pornography, was it? Well, if Mitch reckoned she was
going to knuckle under to his demands, she wasn't the
only one in for a lonely spell.

Reentering her solitary bedroom, she made the V for
victory sign to the mirror above her, then flipped off the

lights. But not before taking one of her male pin-up magazines out of its carton and tucking it under a pillow retrieved from the ignominious pile. Purpose: secret dreams in lieu of spouse, for inspirational purposes only. Of course.

"Are you ever coming out of there, Mommy?" Kevin asked four days later.

"I do come out," Clea replied, looking up from her clattering keyboard, dark circles under her eyes. "It's just that I go right back in again."

Kevin sighed resignedly. "You're nuts, Mom," he said. "And so is Dad."

"Nuts to you, too," Clea teased, her expression lightening a bit. She reached down to pick another reference book off the floor, and when she peered up again, Kevin was gone.

Tanya and Tony had split up, practically at the altar, over a ridiculous disagreement about architectural standards.

It had expanded to such dimensions that they were to debate the matter before a local committee. One word of apology, the slightest willingness to compromise on either side, would have averted disaster. But neither would budge an inch. Verbally, that is.

Tony's calloused hands were at the back of Tanya's neck, kneading the tense muscle that made her wince with pain every time she moved.

Tanya sat on the oak office chair, hunched over, elbows on denim-clad thighs, her face in her hands, crying out softly from time to time as he hit a particularly sensitive area.

As the agony in her neck eased, another agony began, this one from deep within her loins. She hadn't slept with Tony in weeks, had deliberately avoided him, had let

him in this late Friday afternoon only because she was
too weak to protest in the face of his insistence.

It had been a mistake. Her intellect could be as high
and mighty as it wanted, but her sensually deprived body
had its own ideas.

Tony seemed to sense her mounting need, even as she
tried to obliterate it. His amazingly corrupting fingers
moved from her neck to her forehead, massaging her
into compliance.

Then, before she realized it, he was kneeling before
her, a dark-haired god with burning brown eyes that
seemed to sear her very soul.

"Ah," Clea sighed, thrilled at the opportunity to design
yet another love scene. This one would be even better
than the last half dozen, since her own frustrations had
had a dramatic effect on her fantasies.

Six paragraphs and four sentences later her heart was
pounding in anticipation as Tony's sensual massage had
Tanya writhing with unrestrained desire. Clea was so
immersed in her characters that she didn't hear Mitch's
footsteps behind her.

"Where on earth did you learn about that?" he asked.

"Learn about what?" Clea replied lightly, so conscious
of her husband's maleness that she was afraid to turn
around for fear he would see the yearning in her eyes.

"That," Mitch said, reaching over her shoulder and
pointing to a particular sentence in midpage. His hand
brushed her sleeve, and Clea could feel the warmth
spreading through her body. She wanted to take his hand
and kiss it. Instead she said coolly, "Just my writer's
imagination."

"I don't believe you could come up with something
like that unless you'd done it yourself," Mitch stated
unceremoniously.

"Are you accusing me of adultery again?" Clea

snapped, swiveling to face him and then immediately regretting it. Her husband had obviously just come in from playing tennis at the club and was still clad in his white pullover shirt and shorts. Their snug fit emphasized the lines of his ruggedly well-knit body, outlining the muscles of his arms and chest, narrowing to long, sinewy, perfectly shaped legs. His face was still flushed from the exertion and he looked . . . well, gorgeous.

"No, I'm not accusing you of anything," Mitch denied vehemently, staring at her in a visual contest of wills. The warmth Clea had initially felt was now a cauldron brew.

"Then believe what you will," she said, "because this scene is quite pristine compared to some of the others. But, of course, you wouldn't want to read the book yourself. It might corrupt you."

Mitch stood, slowly reading the page she had been typing. Then, just as slowly he studied the top page on top of her manuscript pile. His eyes widened from time to time and he wiped his mouth with the back of his hand.

When he finished his perusal, he reached out as if to flip the top page over and read what was beneath it. Then he checked himself quite abruptly and stated with all apparent disgust, "You're right, I'm not interested."

Clea stared at the bedroom door long after Mitch had slammed it shut behind him.

The next day she added three new books to her reference collection. One of them, written by someone who claimed to be a sex therapist, made Clea's face turn a shade of scarlet that clashed with the bedroom decor.

People just didn't do those things, she decided, though well aware that anything was possible in this world. *This* certainly wasn't romance in any case. It was, well . . . pornography.

With a burst of self-confidence, Clea applied her more

than ample leisure hours to completing her novel, calling up all the tenderness so necessary to the genre. But what if she were to incorporate some of the sex therapist's techniques into the next few chapters—chapters designed specifically for her husband to read?

It was a nasty trick, she mused, five days and one full chapter later. Mitch had barely spoken to her during that time. She had contrived some pretext, late each evening, to leave her room and the burgeoning manuscript unguarded. Upon her return, however, she could never see any sure sign that the pages had been disturbed.

Was Mitch actually reading it? Perhaps he only skimmed her work, making certain she wasn't just typing the alphabet. But there were a number of times when she did catch him gazing at her with the look of a man who had gone to an X-rated movie, only to discover his wife was the "star."

That incredulous expression inspired Clea to even further literary heights. On the fifth evening, having erotically superseded even her wildest dreams, she concealed herself in the bedroom closet, leaving the door open just a bit.

Mitch entered, carefully scanning the room for occupancy. Then he made a beeline for her manuscript, quickly flipping the pages until he came to her most recently completed chapter. This time Mitchell Eduard Bottington didn't blush; he turned absolutely, apoplectically scarlet. Beads of perspiration began to form on his forehead. He loosened his already loose pajama top. His pajama bottom became somewhat snugger. In her darkened seclusion, Clea forced herself not to laugh.

Sunday of the second week, Kevin turned to her at the dinner table and asked glumly, "When is Daddy going to move back in with you?"

"Why?" Clea asked with as much innocence as she could muster, knowing full well that her husband had been pacing the floor each night, well into the wee hours of the morning. She knew this because she was doing the same thing herself, but that was neither here nor there.

"Because he doesn't sleep. He flops around all night," Kevin replied in a disgruntled tone. Then he hesitated, as if unsure whether to continue. The desire to confide won out. "Besides, he's always peeking over to see whether I'm asleep or not. Then he sneaks out and goes into your room. I stay awake till he gets back."

Mitch was carving his steak with an intentness normally reserved for a hole in one on the golf course. As Kevin spoke he gave the knife such a sharp jerk that the piece of sirloin under consideration seemed to leap from the platinum-edged dinner plate onto the carpet. Mitch's reaction was to bury his face in his hands.

Inwardly Clea quit. She couldn't take it anymore. She was miserable. Mitch was miserable. Kevin was miserable. And for what?

"Mitch," she offered softly, "can't we compromise on this?"

"Compromise where?" he responded, looking directly at her now, the harsh edge returning to his voice. "Would you like to wear my trousers? While you're accepting plaudits for your erotic fantasies, will you give a thought to what I'll be going through at Klectronics because of those fantasies? Would you like to be Mitchell Bottington, who has publicly assumed an antismut position, and who has a wife who plans to just as publicly debate him on the issue?"

"I can't always be your shadow," Clea responded, wanting him so much that tears welled up in her eyes.

"What's wrong with being a Bottington?" Mitch asked, strong jaw intransigently clenched. At that moment he looked so much like his father that Clea wondered whether the ghost of the senior Bottington had somehow entered and taken possession of his son's very soul.

"Nothing's wrong with it," Clea replied. "It's just that, as a Bottington, I am, like my beloved husband, entitled to stand up for my beliefs."

"Beloved?" Mitch queried.

"Beloved," Clea reiterated, rising from her chair. "Very much so, or my fight would be a lot easier."

In the ensuing week she wavered a thousand times, a million times, on the brink of capitulation. And then, the afternoon before the debate, the telephone rang.

It was her former landlord. The postal service had been trying to deliver a registered letter. He had copied her telephone number off the "thank you" check Mitch had given him for being so "understanding" about the sudden vacancy of the apartment. Perhaps the letter was important. Perhaps she should go get it.

Clea did. Standing in the post office, minutes before it closed, she stared at the sealed envelope as if in a trance. It bore the return imprint, "Herald Square Press."

Afraid to open it, Clea waited until she arrived home. She turned the envelope over and over, as if there might be some external warning of the message within. Then she held it up to the overhead lamp in the living room, peering through the thick vellum hoping to catch just a few words of the message within. But she could see nothing.

Open it, she told herself. It's not important if the person calls you a fool, and says the writing has the unmistakable touch of an amateur. After all, this was merely a dare, a lark, a way to pass the time for a bored, very wealthy socialite. It had no significance, really.

Watching her hands tremble as she tore open the envelope, Clea knew she was kidding no one. Yes, it had started out as a lark, a dare, but it had turned into a crusade for selfhood. Had she passed the gauntlet or not? Despite her already stiff upper lip, the tiny bird of hope continued to flutter its wings within her heart.

The opening sentence said nothing in particular. Clea read it three times:

> Dear Ms. Veronese,
> I have read your partial manuscript several times.

Clea closed her eyes, opened them, and forced herself to read on.

> As a new editor here at Herald Square Press, I didn't expect to discover such a perfect story for our new line, and from a completely unknown author.

Her knees about to buckle underneath her, Clea managed to find bodily safety in a nearby armchair. The remaining words in the letter practically danced before her eyes:

> We eagerly await the remainder of *Secret Diary of Delights,* which we have tentatively retitled *Passion Most Naked.* A contract will be sent to you in a few weeks, and if you have any questions, please telephone me collect. I would have called you with the good news, but you gave no telephone number and are apparently unlisted.

The letter was signed "Best wishes, Amy Brant." Clea traced the blue-inked signature with her finger, half expecting it to leap off the paper.

Clea sat there listening to the grandfather clock tick the hour away. She let the phone ring unanswered several times, until she realized Kevin had gone to visit a neighborhood friend and the maid had apparently left for the day.

"Hello," she said in a daze. The caller said something, to which she replied, "She's not here. This is Serena Veronese." After which she replaced the receiver, but so crookedly that the connection wasn't broken.

When Mitch slammed through the door an hour later, she was still sitting in the armchair, staring fixedly at her letter.

"What now?" he asked, almost ashen-faced, stalking into the room, but not before he'd adjusted the errant receiver.

Clea's response was to hand him the letter, then place her folded hands in her lap.

As she had read it several times, so did her husband. His expression went from irritation to anger to fury.

"I forbid you," he stated in tones colder and sharper than ice.

"No," Clea replied without discernible emotion, her wide hazel eyes staring into space.

"Did you hear me?" Mitch repeated. "I said that I forbid you to continue this insane and humiliating project."

"It's not insane," Clea replied, her voice soft and almost dreamlike, "and it's not humiliating."

"It's insane to destroy a world that has always provided for you, and provided well. What else do you want that I would not give you? You have only to ask. Test me. Ask me for anything. Another mink coat perhaps? A trip around the world? Diamonds on every finger, and even some for your toes? Just ask. Tell me what it is you want so badly that to get it you would humiliate me in front of my peers. For the humiliation I speak of is mine as well as yours."

Clea stood and faced him, head held high and eyes burning bright. "Self-respect," she said without emotion.

In response Mitch tore her letter in half, then in fourths, then in eighths. Clea didn't wait for the last of the shreds to hit the floor. She marched up the stairs and into her fire-red bedroom, slamming the door behind her. And then, spied upon by mirrors, alone in her round bed, she tried unsuccessfully to stifle her racking sobs in a white satin pillow.

The morning of the debate dawned cool and brilliant. It was one of those midwinter San Francisco days that made it seem as if spring were just around the corner— air crystal clear, sun shining, sea breeze perfumed.

She dressed slowly, each decision on what to wear made with such deliberation that she might have been going to a gala movie premiere instead of a school function. Should she be flamboyant? Artsy? Demure? Appearance counted, no doubt about it, but what image did she want to convey?

The problem, she decided, was that her goals were so mixed. She didn't want to be involved in this debate at all. She wanted her husband to accept her as a professional. But she was a woman, too.

The corners of her mouth turned up ever so slightly, an impish lilt carved on cameo. Anything was possible, after all. How long would Mitch be able to resist their connubial bower?

Even before she had begun her novel, when their techniques were far less exotic—or erotic—her husband had exercised his marital prerogatives with enthusiasm and regularity. Since she had started her research, he had ceased to tiptoe into the bedroom when he returned late at night, coming home considerably earlier and making a great deal of noise in a not-so-subtle effort to wake her up.

And now, for the past three weeks, he had been reading about techniques he probably considered the exclusive preserve of circus acrobats. But then, breathes there a man who doesn't have fantasies? Clea thought not, and the impish lilt broadened into a full-scale grin.

"Kevin," she called out, "what did Daddy wear this morning?"

When her son didn't answer, she had to go track him down. She finally located him in the back yard, where he was trying to get the dog to "beg" for a biscuit reward.

She repeated the question, adding a tailgate of "You'd better hurry or you'll be late for school." Kevin, clad in T-shirt, pajama bottoms, and one untied sneaker, wasn't the least bit worried. School was starting late today, he reminded her. There was some big meeting going on and everybody was running all over the place, "like chickens on Auntie Marion's farm."

Clea finally elicited the information that Daddy was wearing a "dark gray suit, stuffy white shirt, and horrible blood-colored tie. With matching blood-colored socks." He was also wearing a "very grumpy face," like someone who'd swallowed a gum ball without chewing it."

"Maybe he's got acid indigestion," Clea commented blithely, quickly removing herself from the scene before Kevin could ask what "acid suggestion" was.

When completed, her outfit was deliberately meant to mimic her husband's, thus emphasizing her professional status and her equality with him in every way. Her severe dark gray suit was unrelieved by the nurse-white tailored silk blouse underneath. Around her neck was a burgundy silk ribbon tied in an almost masculine bow. She couldn't duplicate the socks, but her shoes were burgundy leather, and her ash-blond hair, pulled tightly back and wound in a chignon, was held at the side with two dark burgundy clasps. A very professional statement, she decided.

Her businesslike image would easily have passed muster at Klectronics headquarters—except for one minor deviation. Clea only hoped that Mitch would be seated within whiffing distance of the $200-an-ounce perfume. Because this particular import would do more than tempt a monk; it would tempt a saint, even a mummified one. Or so she had been promised.

Luck held. Clea ran up the school steps, dashed into the hubbub of the conference room, and found her reserved place at the long tabel. She noted, with some surprise, that she had been seated directly across from her rather stiff-backed and obviously irritated spouse. The most immediate reason for his annoyance was quite obvious to Clea: instead of placing Mitch at the head of the table, as would befit the president of the P.T.L.G., Mrs. DomPeter had taken this most prominent site for herself.

The formidable dowager cast a baleful eye on Clea as she took her place, flanked on either side by two apparently terrified librarians. Mitch, she noted, fared no better. His companions were two starched middle-aged women who looked as if they'd been born and bred in a cardboard factory.

Some jousting match, Clea thought, trying to keep a serious face. We've pitched the fainthearted against those of frail imagination, and are somehow expecting one side to emerge the clear victor.

She tried to catch Mitch's eye. When she finally did, he glared at her. That didn't bother Clea at all. When Mrs. DomPeter slammed her gavel down on the oak table, thereby drawing all eyes in her general direction, Clea blew her husband the barest of kisses. He sat up even straighter and stared at a spot several inches over her head. Clea had to pinch her leg surreptitiously to keep from grinning. Her husband sure was cute when he was angry.

She shuffled the notes she had so carefully prepared, quotes from historical texts on freedom of speech, quotes from erstwhile windy politicians, even some quotes from eminent psychologists and sociologists on the value of imaginative literature as a valuable emotional release mechanism.

Mitch stood and made a brief opening speech. Clea gazed at him worshipfully, aware that the audience's attention was equally divided between the two Bottingtons.

Mitch seemed aware of it too. "This is a difficult day for me," he began, the practiced fire of his approach thrown somewhat off balance because the one responsible for his difficulties was openly contemplating him with the reverence usually reserved for an idol.

He shot her a scathing glance before rapidly moving on to a stern diatribe on the need to foster moral values among the young. "There's time enough for the world to corrupt without our teaching staff helping it out."

Clea thought of Mitch lying stark naked on the oval mahogany table. It was a delicious thought. The deliciousness showed in her wide, long-lashed hazel eyes. Perhaps her husband picked up on this, because his jaw tightened perceptibly. Just to make sure, when Mitch finally took his seat again, Clea welcomed him by tickling his ankle with one nylon-clad toe.

Mitch tugged at his tie, ostensibly straightening it, but actually loosening the knot to give himself more free breathing space. Clea smiled as if they were in collusion. Mitch stared down at the pile of papers in front of him and randomly began to shuffle them. Every time he glanced up, he saw Clea smiling at him. After a while he didn't look up. But he didn't move his leg either.

Clea studied her husband's face carefully as the two cardboard figures on either side of him mumbled their precise, prepared speeches. She reviewed his tanned, smooth forehead with just the beginnings of worry lines. Her eyes caressed his dark, arched brows, the firm cheekbones, the angular line of his jaw. She lingered over his mouth, loving the way it had just the slightest of upward tilts even when he was being perfectly stern. As now.

"Mrs. Bottington, are you awake?"

Coming out of her pleasant reverie with a start of astonishment, Clea abruptly reached out for her own stack of notes. To her horror, the back of her hand hit the water glass. Careening across the Formica table, it turned over on Mitch's lap after generously dousing the woman sitting next to him.

"Oh my, oh my," the woman shrieked, jumping up as Clea leaned over to apologize profusely. Mitch offered the woman his handkerchief, and soon she sat back down, dabbing at her bodice while continuing to mutter to herself.

Mitch never flinched—even though, Clea now saw, a pile of ice cubes resided in his lap.

"Can I dry you off?" she whispered, leaning over to give him a scented lacy handkerchief from her purse. Her hand brushed his, ever so accidentally, sending shivers up her spine, shivers that would have melted the most resilient of ice cubes, she thought breathlessly.

"No," Mitch said, mouthing the word rather than saying it aloud. After the briefest of instants he also mouthed, "And cut out the clown act."

Giving him the most innocent of looks, Clea started fiddling with her burgundy silk surrogate necktie. Mitch winced, recognizing the gesture as one of his own. Clea grinned, then pulled her chair so far forward that she could touch his damp knee with her toe. As she poked his knee, Mitch looked up at the ceiling. Clea grinned again.

"Mrs. Bottington, I do hope you consider this a serious matter and not a joke."

"Mrs. DomPeter, I have much more at stake here than you do."

"That's hard to believe . . . my dear. But, if you can

keep clear of the water glass, we're willing to listen."

Mrs. DomPeter's glare was so acerbic that at almost any other time or place Clea might well have been cowed by it. But now, with Mitch looking on, his sea-gray eyes more curious than anything else, Clea barely noticed it.

She reached for her notes and then, on impulse, turned them face down instead. She didn't need notes to remind her of what had to be communicated.

"Once upon a time," she began clearly, "I too would have condemned anything that I hadn't experienced within the boundaries of the sheltered world in which I was raised. That time was not so long ago.

"By refusing, for whatever reasons, to expand my horizons, I eventually found that I could not learn. It took me some time to realize this. Nobody cared, not even myself. I had a successful husband and that was all that mattered.

"Or so I thought. But after a while, I ceased to find that fulfilling. My husband's success was not mine, any more than the beauty of an individual can be credited to the mirror which reflects that individual—"

"Mrs. Bottington," Mrs. DomPeter broke in, "whether or not you respect your husband's multiple achievements is not at question in this debate. If you would confine yourself to the subject at hand—in this case filthy reading material for our children—it would be appreciated."

"I'd appreciate it if you would let my wife finish what she's saying without interruption," Mitch stated clearly enough to be heard by everybody in the room.

Someone applauded and Mrs. DomPeter pursed her lips, appearing extraordinarily like a toad who had consumed a batch of stinging nettles instead of a juicy insect.

Clea gave her husband a smile of pure gratitude. His eyes crinkled at the corners and his mouth tilted upward a bit more.

Taking a deep breath, she proceeded, flinging caution

to the wind. "The thing about 'filthy' reading material is that if you read it, all of it, instead of selected passages taken out of context, sometimes you actually find a good story. Sometimes you even find a moral story."

"I doubt that, my dear," Mrs. DomPeter interjected caustically, as the cardboard figures on either side of Mitch nodded assent.

Clea swiveled and faced the supremely quiet audience. "Do you remember reading the following books as a child?" she asked. *"Huckleberry Finn, Alice's Adventures in Wonderland, Robinson Crusoe?"*

There were nods of assent and Clea forced herself to speak in the clear, ringing tones of truth. "And how many of you out there have read *Gone With the Wind?*" she inquired, lifting her arm as if to invite a visible reply.

It came, with two-thirds of the audience raising their hands in witness.

"There's *The Old Man and the Sea,*" said one librarian.

"And Shakespeare's *The Merchant of Venice,*" the other librarian chimed in.

Mrs. DomPeter looked as if she were about to choke on a lump of beeswax. Clea ignored her. Instead she turned toward the audience one final time and asked, "Is there any person here who would be willing to stand up and condemn *The American Heritage Dictionary?*"

No one moved. Clea continued. "All these books have, at one time or another, been labeled 'decadent.' Tell me, Mrs. DomPeter, what's decadent about *Alice in Wonderland?*"

The dowager's eyes shot daggers in Clea's direction, but she made no response.

"I don't believe in censorship," Clea stated in a softer tone. "You start censoring one thing and then it's the next thing, and soon enough we won't have any libraries or book stores or magazine racks.

"If every book that depicted love scenes between consenting adults was banned . . ." Clea paused, hearing the
palpable hush that came over the audience at the same
time she saw warning flags go up all over her husband's
face. "If all were banned, I wouldn't have had the opportunity to read the delightful romance novel left behind
in my kitchen by my very fastidious—and incidentally,
very moral—cleaning woman. Nor would I have had
the opportunity to write and sell a romance of my own.
Which I have just done."

Reporters and photographers seemed to spring from
nowhere, cameras clicking. One particularly intrepid
young man leaped onto the stage, his flash attachment
held so close to her face that Clea flinched.

"Tell me, Mrs. Bottington," the reporter shouted,
practically in Clea's ear, "Why would a millionaire's
wife stoop to writing pornography?"

That the reporter's nose wasn't rearranged by Mitch's
fist was due only to the former's swiftness. For a moment
it appeared that Mitch would chase him into the aisles,
but then his shoulders squared with restraint and he sat
down again, fists clenched into knuckle-whitened balls.

Mrs. DomPeter was banging on the table with her oak
gavel, the pounding ceasing only when the gavel snapped
in two. After which she pounded, just as futilely, with
her fist.

Clea was still standing. When the uproar diminished
slightly, she said into the microphone, "I assure you, it's
a very good book," and took her seat again.

Mitch, elbows on table, lowered his head to his whitened knuckles.

Ignoring the two librarians who were glancing at Clea
with marked admiration, Mrs. DomPeter got to her feet
and began to speak. Her first words proclaimed the evils

of sex of all varieties; and she went on from there to denounce the even greater evil of discussing such a vile topic in a public forum.

For a few minutes Mitch seemed bored, then perplexed, then actually interested.

"What are you thinking about?" Clea wrote on a piece of paper which she slid across the table.

"This is not the appropriate time to discuss it," Mitch wrote back.

"Why?" Clea penned, much to the consternation of the librarians on either side of her. Both turned to peer at Mitch, as though awaiting his response.

"Mr. Bottington," Mrs. DomPeter said, drawing herself up to full puff-pigeon height. "Far be it from me to criticize the public manners of a man who runs a business empire."

Mitch shifted his chair so it faced the head of the table and he sat so casually, eyes somnolently lidded, dark lashes shading his chiseled cheekbones, that it surely seemed to the uninitiated in the audience that he would take this chastisement as his just due.

Observing the tiniest of perceptible twitches in his jaw, Clea knew this wasn't so. A colleague of Mitch's had once told her that when, in the midst of contract negotiations, Mitch seemed to be going to sleep, then everybody involved should be careful. Unfortunately Mrs. DomPeter didn't know this.

"You joined our worthy P.T.L.G. of your own volition," she stated with a satisfied grimace, punctuating it with two croupy smoker's coughs. "You stated publicly that you wanted our hallowed classrooms free of the type of trash that feeds on the mind. Smutty books. Therefore, we had every reason to expect your support." She held her hand up toward the audience as if to silence potential applause.

By now Mitch appeared to be in sandman's heaven.

Not a muscle moved, except for that almost nonexistent twitch in his cheek. Clea's eyes were focused on it as if drawn by a magnet.

"Instead," Mrs. DomPeter continued haughtily, "you seem to be deliberately ignoring the proceedings we so carefully planned. In lieu of paying attention, you are passing concealed notes across the table to your wife— your wife, a woman who has forgotten her very excellent upbringing and who has come here to make a mockery of our group by announcing she has written a book about the sins of the flesh. I won't ask her to apologize. But you can, if you wish, apologize for the two of you."

The room was so still they might have been in a cavern, fathoms beneath the earth. Clea stood, hands gripping the table for support but head held high.

"My husband doesn't have to apologize for me," she stated firmly. "I will do that on my own. I had no right to hold my husband up to ridicule because of a book he did not know I'd written. I should have turned down your invitation, Mrs. DomPeter. Because I did not have the wisdom to do so, I now offer my regrets for my unseemly behavior this morning."

Just as a derisive smile of triumph began to spread across Mrs. DomPeter's face, Mitch stood up. His commanding presence was such that he would have dominated any international boardroom or major political caucus.

"Ridiculous," he said uncharacteristically as the cameras flashed again. "My wife certainly does not offer her regrets. Do you, Clea?"

He scrutinized her as she stood there, daring her to disobey.

"Well..." she began, not quiet sure how to proceed.

"Well?" he repeated, pinioning her with a glare that far outstripped anything Mrs. DomPeter could possibly offer.

"Well, I guess I apologize for my apology," Clea stated with such honest bewilderment that someone in the audience tittered sympathetically.

"That's better," Mitch stated authoritatively.

"Oh, I . . . I . . . good," Clea stammered, feeling more the fool with each passing minute.

"I can see my wife is somewhat overwhelmed by all this unrelenting attention," Mitch said protectively. "But it's nothing compared to the attention that will come her way once the heartwarming romance she has written is actually published."

Clea's eyebrows went full arch. Heartwarming?

Mitch grinned, white teeth flashing in his wide, sensuous mouth, agate eyes issuing a merry challenge. "I assure you," he pronounced distinctly, "that my wife's book is a true delight. In fact, I am so confirmed in this judgment that, when the book comes out, I shall purchase copies for every person who attended this P.T.L.G meeting. Then you all can make your own judgment."

Deciding she would faint from shock if she didn't sit down immediately, Clea did just that.

Mitch turned full face to the audience, exuding so much charisma that people began to clamber on stage just to shake his hand in congratulation. Amidst the uproar, Clea turned to check Mrs. DomPeter's reaction. However, the formidable dowager was nowhere to be seen.

When her head had finally stopped spinning, Clea discovered her husband had moved to the exit of the room, where he was shaking hands with the room's final two occupants. These happened to be the librarians.

"Do let us know when your novel comes out," they chorused, practically in unison. "We'll display it prominently on our main shelf."

Mustering up her remaining strength, Clea just smiled at them, hoping her confusion didn't show. It was all too much, too fast, too soon.

She managed to rise from the chair, her burgundy heels clicking as she walked gingerly across the polished floor.

Mitch loosened his tie, unbuttoned the top of his shirt, and leaned back against the wall, hands in pockets, long legs crossed in front of him.

Shamefaced, Clea touched his chest lightly, then started to walk on through the door. "Where are you going?" Mitch asked.

"Home," Clea replied, her senses still in a whirl.

"Wait a minute. I have a great idea for your novel—another romantic episode. It takes place in a cloistered schoolroom with Mrs. DomPeter lurking outside."

"Mitchell Eduard Bottington, don't you start—" Clea warned.

"I didn't start it, you did."

"I am going home, Mitchell. Right now."

"An excellent idea," he retorted with a leer.

"What on earth are you suggesting?" Clea asked in exasperation.

"A little tête-à-tête in bed," he said promptly. "I'd like to suggest that we..." He bent over and whispered the rest of the sentence in her ear.

Somewhere within the blur of Clea's mind was the recognition that her husband had borrowed considerably from Tony's erotic vocabulary. When Tony had spoken those words, Clea's heroine had blushed. Now, however, it was her true-life hero who was blushing.

Clea started to laugh, light, floating laughter that bounced off the walls of the empty room.

"I hope you realize what you're getting into," Clea warned indulgently, looping her arm under his jacket and around his waist.

"I hope you realize what you've just said," Mitch retorted, reaching up to take the pins out of her chignon, allowing her golden hair to flow freely across her shoulders.

"I was referring to my book," Clea said languidly, as she rubbed her fingers affectionately over the small of his back. "I've got to finish it."

"All in good time," Mitch countered, bending to kiss Clea's forehead in full view of the teachers and pupils remaining in the corridor.

But by the time they had reached Hampstead Estates, Mitch's mood had apparently changed. The demonic glint in his eyes was barely perceptible.

"Back to the typewriter, dear wife," he ordered, not very gruffly.

Clea, who during the drive home from the school had been daydreaming about joining Mitch in their bedroom, felt suddenly crushed.

But in the end, more curious than obedient, she sat down at her typewriter, removed her jacket, and placed her fingers on the keys. "Now what?" she asked.

"Tony will say this to Tanya," Mitch instructed, whispering the words in her ear.

With eyes like saucers, Clea typed out the sentences Mitch dictated. "Are you sure Tony's come off his macho horse sufficiently to accept Tanya as both a competent *and* a feminine woman?" she asked.

"The strength of a good man does not lie solely in his muscles," Mitch stated, then pointed to the typewriter and gestured that Clea should add that to what she had just typed.

"Now what will Tanya say?" Clea inquired, getting into the spirit of the game.

"Oh," Mitch noted, "she will promise him this . . ." Again he whispered in Clea's ear, managing to nibble on it in the process.

"Oh," murmured Clea, embarrassed at having to write

such endearments with her husband peering over her shoulder.

"Tony will be encouraged that Tanya is willing to meet him halfway," Mitch added in a professorial tone. "So he will say..." And again Mitch whispered the words. Again his tongue dipped into her ear, causing a new stream of shivers to run down her spine.

Her fingers clicking away at the keyboard, Clea paused briefly to glance up and ask, "Why are you whispering?"

"I don't want anybody to overhear me encouraging you to write pornography," Mitch responded with a poker face.

"But there's nothing pornographic about this," Clea protested. "It's just what we romance writers euphemistically call 'sensual.'"

"But we've barely begun," Mitch informed her matter-of-factly. "After all, this is their prehoneymoon scene."

"Prehoneymoon?" Clea said, puzzled.

"They're going to apply for a marriage license as soon as our hero regains his strength," Mitch amplified.

"Regains his strength?" Clea responded. "Why should he need to do that?"

"Perhaps I should act out the next couple of pages for you," Mitch offered generously, removing his jacket and starting to unbutton his shirt.

Clea felt a familiar pleasurable prickle. It started at the back of her neck and worked its way down to her toes.

The next morning, rather late, Clea rose to finish the chapter. Writing love scenes, she mused, humming softly to herself, was a piece of cake.

NEW FROM THE PUBLISHERS OF *SECOND CHANCE AT LOVE*!

To Have and to Hold

___	**THE TESTIMONY #1** Robin James	06928-0
___	**A TASTE OF HEAVEN #2** Jennifer Rose	06929-9
___	**TREAD SOFTLY #3** Ann Cristy	06930-2
___	**THEY SAID IT WOULDN'T LAST #4** Elaine Tucker	06931-0
___	**GILDED SPRING #5** Jenny Bates	06932-9
___	**LEGAL AND TENDER #6** Candice Adams	06933-7
___	**THE FAMILY PLAN #7** Nuria Wood	06934-5
___	**HOLD FAST 'TIL DAWN #8** Mary Haskell	06935-3
___	**HEART FULL OF RAINBOWS #9** Melanie Randolph	06936-1
___	**I KNOW MY LOVE #10** Vivian Connolly	06937-X
___	**KEYS TO THE HEART #11** Jennifer Rose	06938-8
___	**STRANGE BEDFELLOWS #12** Elaine Tucker	06939-6
___	**MOMENTS TO SHARE #13** Katherine Granger	06940-X
___	**SUNBURST #14** Jeanne Grant	06941-8
___	**WHATEVER IT TAKES #15** Cally Hughes	06942-6
___	**LADY LAUGHING EYES #16** Lee Damon	06943-4
___	**ALL THAT GLITTERS #17** Mary Haskell	06944-2
___	**PLAYING FOR KEEPS #18** Elissa Curry	06945-0
___	**PASSION'S GLOW #19** Marilyn Brian	06946-9
___	**BETWEEN THE SHEETS #20** Tricia Adams	06947-7
___	**MOONLIGHT AND MAGNOLIAS #21** Vivian Connolly	06948-5
___	**A DELICATE BALANCE #22** Kate Wellington	06949-3

All Titles are $1.95

Prices may be slightly higher in Canada.

Available at your local bookstore or return this form to:

 SECOND CHANCE AT LOVE
Book Mailing Service
P.O. Box 690, Rockville Centre, NY 11571

Please send me the titles checked above. I enclose _____ Include 75¢ for postage and handling if one book is ordered; 25¢ per book for two or more not to exceed $1.75. California, Illinois, New York and Tennessee residents please add sales tax.

NAME_____

ADDRESS_____

CITY_____ STATE/ZIP_____
(allow six weeks for delivery)   **THTH #67**

WATCH FOR 6 NEW TITLES EVERY MONTH!

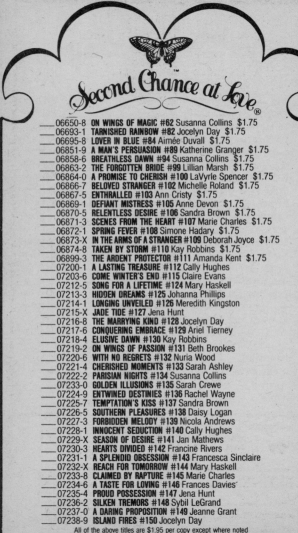

Second Chance at Love ®

___ 06650-8	ON WINGS OF MAGIC #62 Susanna Collins	$1.75
___ 06693-1	TARNISHED RAINBOW #82 Jocelyn Day	$1.75
___ 06695-8	LOVER IN BLUE #84 Aimée Duvall	$1.75
___ 06851-9	A MAN'S PERSUASION #89 Katherine Granger	$1.75
___ 06858-6	BREATHLESS DAWN #94 Susanna Collins	$1.75
___ 06863-2	THE FORGOTTEN BRIDE #99 Lillian Marsh	$1.75
___ 06864-0	A PROMISE TO CHERISH #100 LaVyrle Spencer	$1.75
___ 06866-7	BELOVED STRANGER #102 Michelle Roland	$1.75
___ 06867-5	ENTHRALLED #103 Ann Cristy	$1.75
___ 06869-1	DEFIANT MISTRESS #105 Anne Devon	$1.75
___ 06870-5	RELENTLESS DESIRE #106 Sandra Brown	$1.75
___ 06871-3	SCENES FROM THE HEART #107 Marie Charles	$1.75
___ 06872-1	SPRING FEVER #108 Simone Hadary	$1.75
___ 06873-X	IN THE ARMS OF A STRANGER #109 Deborah Joyce	$1.75
___ 06874-8	TAKEN BY STORM #110 Kay Robbins	$1.75
___ 06899-3	THE ARDENT PROTECTOR #111 Amanda Kent	$1.75
___ 07200-1	A LASTING TREASURE #112 Cally Hughes	
___ 07203-6	COME WINTER'S END #115 Claire Evans	
___ 07212-5	SONG FOR A LIFETIME #124 Mary Haskell	
___ 07213-3	HIDDEN DREAMS #125 Johanna Phillips	
___ 07214-1	LONGING UNVEILED #126 Meredith Kingston	
___ 07215-X	JADE TIDE #127 Jena Hunt	
___ 07216-8	THE MARRYING KIND #128 Jocelyn Day	
___ 07217-6	CONQUERING EMBRACE #129 Ariel Tierney	
___ 07218-4	ELUSIVE DAWN #130 Kay Robbins	
___ 07219-2	ON WINGS OF PASSION #131 Beth Brookes	
___ 07220-6	WITH NO REGRETS #132 Nuria Wood	
___ 07221-4	CHERISHED MOMENTS #133 Sarah Ashley	
___ 07222-2	PARISIAN NIGHTS #134 Susanna Collins	
___ 07233-0	GOLDEN ILLUSIONS #135 Sarah Crewe	
___ 07224-9	ENTWINED DESTINIES #136 Rachel Wayne	
___ 07225-7	TEMPTATION'S KISS #137 Sandra Brown	
___ 07226-5	SOUTHERN PLEASURES #138 Daisy Logan	
___ 07227-3	FORBIDDEN MELODY #139 Nicola Andrews	
___ 07228-1	INNOCENT SEDUCTION #140 Cally Hughes	
___ 07229-2	SEASON OF DESIRE #141 Jan Mathews	
___ 07230-3	HEARTS DIVIDED #142 Francine Rivers	
___ 07231-1	A SPLENDID OBSESSION #143 Francesca Sinclaire	
___ 07232-X	REACH FOR TOMORROW #144 Mary Haskell	
___ 07233-8	CLAIMED BY RAPTURE #145 Marie Charles	
___ 07234-6	A TASTE FOR LOVING #146 Frances Davies	
___ 07235-4	PROUD POSSESSION #147 Jena Hunt	
___ 07236-2	SILKEN TREMORS #148 Sybil LeGrand	
___ 07237-0	A DARING PROPOSITION #149 Jeanne Grant	
___ 07238-9	ISLAND FIRES #150 Jocelyn Day	

All of the above titles are $1.95 per copy except where noted

SK-41a

All of the above titles are $1.95
Prices may be slightly higher in Canada.

Available at your local bookstore or return this form to:

SECOND CHANCE AT LOVE
Book Mailing Service
P.O. Box 690, Rockville Centre, NY 11571

Please send me the titles checked above. I enclose _____. Include 75¢ for postage and handling if one book is ordered; 25¢ per book for two or more not to exceed $1.75. California, Illinois, New York and Tennessee residents please add sales tax.

NAME _____

ADDRESS _____

CITY _____ STATE/ZIP_____

(allow six weeks for delivery)   **SK-41b**

HERE'S WHAT READERS ARE SAYING ABOUT

To Have and to Hold™

"Your TO HAVE AND TO HOLD series is
a fabulous and long overdue idea."
—*A. D., Upper Darby, PA**

"I have been reading romance novels for over
ten years and feel the TO HAVE AND TO HOLD
series is the best I have read. It's exciting,
sensitive, refreshing, well written. Many thanks
for a series of books I can relate to."
—*O. K., Bensalem, PA**

"I enjoy your books tremendously."
—*J. C., Houston, TX**

"I love the books and read them over and over."
—*E. K., Warren, MI**

"You have another winner with the new TO HAVE
AND TO HOLD series."
—*R. P., Lincoln Park, MI**

"I love the new series TO HAVE AND TO HOLD."
—*M. L., Cleveland, OH**

"I've never written a fan letter before, but
TO HAVE AND TO HOLD is fantastic."
—*E. S., Narberth, PA**

*Name and address available upon request